D1738460

THE HORSE SOLDIER

THE HORSE SOLDIER

ETHAN J. WOLFE

THORNDIKE PRESS
A part of Gale, a Cengage Company

Copyright © 2021 by Ethan J. Wolfe.
Thorndike Press, a part of Gale, a Cengage Company.

Thorndike Press® Large Print Western.
The text of this Large Print edition is unabridged.
Other aspects of the book may vary from the original edition.
Set in 16 pt. Plantin.

LIBRARY OF CONGRESS CIP DATA ON FILE.
CATALOGUING IN PUBLICATION FOR THIS BOOK
IS AVAILABLE FROM THE LIBRARY OF CONGRESS.

ISBN-13: 978-1-4328-7112-3 (hardcover alk. paper)

Published in 2021 by arrangement with Ethan J. Wolfe

Printed in Mexico
Print Number: 01   Print Year: 2022

THE HORSE SOLDIER

CHAPTER ONE

Washington, D.C., 1901

At his desk in the US Marshal's building in Washington, D.C., Glen Post read a report that disturbed him greatly.

At sixty years of age, Post would retire in one more year, sometime in the summer of 1902. For now, he would continue his duties as deputy director of the US Marshal's Service, a position he'd held for almost a decade.

Some of his duties included oversight of the divisions of field offices, of which there were many.

Many and not enough. When he was a young man, the population of the USA was a bit more than thirty million. The census of 1900 put the population at nearly eighty million. While the population had nearly tripled, the number of marshals had not.

The report out of Laramie, Wyoming, was quite disturbing in its contents. It would require some straightening out — and soon. Left unchecked, the situation would become disastrous.

The question rolling around in Post's mind was, what should be the proper course of action to take to resolve the situation? For the service and for the citizens of Laramie.

He decided to study the situation over lunch. He left his office, told his secretary where he would be, and then walked several blocks to his favorite restaurant on the Hill. It was his favorite restaurant not for the food, although that was quite good, but for the ambience it provided.

The restaurant was a gathering place for congressmen, senators, their staff, reporters, and other Washington officials. The best place for a reporter to acquire off-the-record information and Washington gossip was over lunch at the restaurant. The only way for a non-player such as himself to get a table was to arrive there exactly at noon when the doors opened and hope for the best.

By twelve-fifteen, every table and seat at the bar would be occupied. Usually Post was amused by the whirling gossip and under-the-table deals, but today he paid no mind to any of it.

He sleepwalked through lunch as he

mulled over various options. By dessert, he was sure about what he would do.

When he returned to his office, Post stopped at his secretary's desk.

"I need you to run an errand for me when you go to lunch," Post said. "Take as much time as you like, but go to the railroad station and pick up a round-trip ticket for me to Miles City in Montana."

"Shall I put it on the service's account?" the secretary said.

"No, I'll pay for it myself," Post said and dipped into his wallet.

"Yes, sir."

"Oh, and have the ticket delivered to my home," Post said. "I need to go home and pack."

"Yes, sir," the secretary said.

Chapter Two

Montana, 1901, Spring

Shirtless, sweat dripping off his chest and arms, Sam Tillman's torso appeared to be carved out of wood as he slammed a posthole digger into the earth.

At the age of sixty, after a lifetime of hard work, Tillman's body appeared half its age. He stood six-two in his stocking feet, six inches above the average height of a man in his day.

His sandy-colored hair was speckled with gray, especially around the temples. His blue eyes were sharp and clear, even if the need to wear spectacles when reading in very dim light became normal after he turned fifty.

Tillman paused for a few seconds to look at his sons, who were also digging postholes. Glen, the elder of the two, was tall and broad like his father, but had darker hair and brown eyes.

Jake, sixteen months younger than his

brother, was slim like his mother and possessed her good looks, fair hair, and gray eyes.

Both of his sons were hardened by years of toiling on the ranch and unspoiled by the simple lifestyle they led as cattle ranchers in Montana.

As he drove the posthole digger into the dirt, Jake said, "Hey, Pop, the lunch my wife brought us is getting cold."

"What did she bring us?" Tillman said.

"Fried chicken, potato salad, apple pie, and cold milk," Jake said. "And some apples for a snack."

"Fried chicken is best eaten cold, but I suppose we can take a break and have us a bite," Tillman said.

Tillman slammed the posthole digger into the ground and removed his gloves. Glen and Jake did the same. Then they walked over to the supply wagon, where a towel covered a large picnic basket on the front seat.

Tillman removed the towel. "Boys, let's eat," he said.

Jake carried the basket to the shade of a nearby tree, and they feasted on chicken, potato salad, and cold milk from a thermos.

"How far do you want to go today, Pop?" Glen asked.

"As far as we can go before an hour before sunset," Tillman said.

Glen and Jake looked at the posts and fencing in the wagon. "We might run out before then, Pop," Glen said.

"Plenty in the barn to start over tomorrow if we do," Tillman said.

"We were afraid you were going to say that," Jake said.

"A little hard work getting you down, Jake," Tillman said.

"Come on, Pop," Jake said.

"How's that apple pie doing?" Tillman said.

Glen used the knife in the basket to slice into the pie. "Let's find out," he said.

Within minutes, the pie and milk were gone, and the three men returned to work. Digging postholes was brutal on the arms, shoulders, and back, but if the heavy toil bothered Tillman, he didn't show it.

Glen and Jake stopped several times to grab sips of water, but Tillman kept right on working until Jake brought him the canteen. Only then did he pause to take a few sips and wipe sweat off his brow.

As Jake returned the canteen to the wagon, he looked down the road and said, "Hey, Pop, someone is coming. Looks like a buggy."

Without pausing to look up, Tillman drove the posthole digger into the dirt and said, "I spotted him a while ago. He's still a ways off."

Jake returned to digging postholes.

After a few minutes, Tillman looked at Jake. "Jake, ride over to my house and tell my sister to set a formal table for tonight. Then get your wife and kids and bring them over. Glen, you do the same," he said.

"Why, Pop? Who's coming?" Glen said.

"Yeah, Pop, who is in that buggy?" Jake said.

Tillman gave Jake his look, the one that reduced Jake to the boy he knew he still was, compared to his father.

"Sure, Pop, right away," Jake said.

Jake went to his horse, which was tethered to the rear of the wagon, put on the saddle, mounted up, and rode off to the northern section of the ranch where his home was located.

Tillman and Glen continued digging postholes until Glen paused to look down the road. "Pop, that buggy will be here any minute."

Tillman looked down the road, and then gave the posthole digger a final whack into the dirt.

"That's it for today, Glen," Tillman said

and walked to the wagon and picked up his shirt.

Glen watched as the buggy arrived and stopped beside the wagon. Post looked at Glen and nodded.

"Remember me, son?" Post said.

"I'm sorry, sir, I do not," Glen said.

Tucking in his shirt, the round US Marshal's badge pinned on the left pocket, Tillman walked to the buggy.

"Son, this is the deputy director of the Marshal's Service, Glen Post. You were named for this man," Tillman said.

Glen looked at Post. "It's an honor to meet you, sir," he said.

Post stepped down from the buggy and shook hands with Glen. "Last time I saw you was back in eighty-one at your mother's funeral. That was a hard time for all of us, I'm afraid," Post said.

"Yes, sir, it was," Glen said.

Tillman stood next to Glen. "So, Deputy Director Post, have you come all the way from Washington, D.C., just to give me my gold watch?" he said.

Post smiled. "Not for twenty-eight more days. Then we figure to bring you and the entire family to Washington for some big doings," he said.

"You didn't come all the way from Washington, the last thirty miles in a buggy, just to tell me that," Tillman said. "Did you?"

"Sam, we need to talk," Post said. "Privately."

"No secrets in my family. Anything you tell me I'm just going to tell them later," Tillman said. "So take the short way through the barn and spell it out. It'll save us all some time."

Post sighed and shook his head. "Have it your way, Sam. That man you appointed town marshal in Laramie is causing some problems. The mess is going to need some straightening out, and soon," he said.

Tillman nodded. "I've heard some rumblings," he said.

"Rumblings? The entire town's sheriff's department has quit. He runs the town like he was the Czar of Russia. He has five deputies, and they all carry shotguns on patrol. The people are . . ." Post said.

Tillman waved his right hand. "We'll talk about it after supper. Right now, let's get you to the house where you can wash up," he said. "You got enough dust on you to fill a sandbag."

Post slapped some dust off his jacket. "I suppose I could use some tidying up," he said.

"A bit," Tillman said as he walked to his

massive horse and grabbed the saddle from the wagon.

"Still a horse soldier, aren't you, Sam?" Post said.

As he strapped on the saddle, Tillman said, "Old habits, I'm afraid."

Glen looked at Post. "What was that you just called my father?" he said.

Post raised an eyebrow. "Do you mean to tell me you don't know about your father?" he said.

"Know what, sir?" Glen said.

"Never mind about that now, son. Go home and fetch your family," Tillman said. "And change your shirt. You're a sight."

"Yes, sir," Glen said.

Glen stepped up into the wagon and took the reins. "See you directly, Pop. Mr. Post," he said and rode toward the southern range, where his home was located.

Tillman mounted the saddle.

"Where's your Colt, Sam?" Post said.

"I don't need to go heeled to ride my own land. Now try and keep up. That nag you rented doesn't look like he's got another mile or two left in him. Maybe," Tillman said.

With a tug of the reins, Tillman rode his horse west.

Post rushed to his buggy. "Wait for me, Sam," he said.

CHAPTER THREE

Tillman dismounted at the corral in front of his home. His younger sister by three years, Alice, was shucking peas on the front porch.

"You might have given me some advance warning," Alice said.

"I did. I sent Jake," Tillman said.

Alice shook her head. "An hour isn't enough time to prepare to entertain company," she said. "And speaking of company, where is he?"

Tillman turned around as Post arrived in his buggy.

"Just leave it, Glen," Tillman said. "I'll see to the horses in a bit."

Post stepped down from the buggy, and he and Tillman went up to the porch.

"Alice, do you remember Mr. Post?" Tillman said.

"Of course, I do," Alice said. "How are you, Mr. Post?"

"Very well, Alice," Post said.

"Pull up a chair while I get us something cold to drink," Tillman said.

Tillman entered the house, and Post took the chair beside Alice.

Alice glared at him for a few moments. "Why don't you people leave him alone? Hasn't he done enough for you people wearing a badge?" she said.

Post did his best to appear innocent. "Rest assured, Alice. I'm not here for anything like that. This is a simple formality," he said.

Alice violently snapped a peapod. "And you came all the way from Washington for a simple formality," she said. "A telegram would have accomplished that very thing."

"I owe it to Sam to talk to him in person," Post said.

Tillman returned with two tall glasses of lemonade over ice and handed one to Post.

Post looked at his glass. "Ice. Wherever did you get ice in the middle of spring way out here?" he said.

Tillman sipped his lemonade. "No shortage of ice in Montana. We grow it six months out of the year, wrap it in burlap, and then stick it in an icehouse for the summer months," he said.

Post sampled the lemonade. "Excellent," he said.

"Alice, I've invited the entire brood for supper," Tillman said.

"Jake told me," Alice said. "And I require more than a few minutes' warning, thank you."

Tillman grinned. "Relax, Alice. The womenfolk will help you. If need be, so will the menfolk," he said.

"As if I would ever allow you in my kitchen," Alice said.

"I've cooked a chicken or two in my time," Tillman said.

Alice set the basket of peapods aside and stood up. "Not in my kitchen, you haven't," she said, opened the door, and entered the house.

Tillman took Alice's chair. "So, how bad a situation is it for you to come all the way from Washington, D.C., when a telegram would accomplish the same thing?" he said.

Post sipped from his glass and then set it on the small table between the chairs. "Bad, I'm afraid. Laramie is a very important town, Sam. It's the hub of the Central Pacific Railroad next to Cheyenne, and the marshal's got the entire town buffaloed. The word I got is he doesn't so much as enforce the laws, but make his own," he said. "And those who object to his laws pay a heavy penalty."

Tillman shook his head. "I heard some things, but nothing as severe as what you just said," he said.

Post looked at Tillman, hesitated, and then said, "I'm sending territorial marshal Ralph Waldo and six deputies to Laramie to remove him. They should arrive within a week."

Tillman set his glass on the table beside Post's. "How in the world do you run off an entire sheriff's department?" he said.

"With bloodshed, Sam," Post said. "And a lot of it."

Tillman sighed heavily. "I'm sorry it came to this," he said.

"Don't be. It's not the first time an appointed man went bad, and it won't be the last," Post said. "It's just the nature of things."

Tillman sighed and then stood up. "Hot water is boiling for your bath. Get cleaned up before supper. My boys and their brood will be here shortly," he said.

In the living room, after Post refreshed himself and changed into a fresh suit, Tillman made the introductions.

"May I present Glen's wife, Sarah, and their three daughters: Rebecca, Alice, and Sarah. This is Jake's wife, Linda, and their two daughters, Alice and Mary. Everybody, this is Mr. Glen Post from Washington, D.C.," Tillman said.

Post looked at all the children. "What a fine-looking bunch of young women," he said.

"A boy or two wouldn't hurt none," Tillman said.

"Aw, Pop," Glen said.

Jake's daughter Alice looked up at Post. "I'm the oldest," she said.

Tillman picked up the girl, kissed her on the cheek, and said, "And that means you have the honor of entertaining Mr. Post while I go change for supper."

Tillman set Alice down, and she looked at Post. "Grandpa means you get to sit with me," she said.

"It shall be my distinct honor," Post said.

Alice appeared from the kitchen. "You men get out of my hair and wait on the porch until supper is ready," she said. "I'll bring out some coffee."

Post, Glen, and Jake sat in chairs on the porch. Each had a cup of coffee.

"This is a fine place, this ranch," Post said.

"It's taken some work to get it where it is," Jake said. "It's all me and Glen know how to do, this ranch."

"Mr. Post, may I ask you a question?" Glen said.

"Of course," Post said.

"Earlier you referred to my father as a horse soldier. What did you mean by that?" Glen said.

Post looked at Glen and Jake for a moment. "Don't you boys know about your father?" he said. "The things he's done?"

Glen shook his head. "I'm afraid our father isn't the most talkative of men, Mr. Post," he said. "Especially about his past."

Post took a sip of his coffee and then looked at Glen and Jake. "That tall horse he always rides is an old habit he acquired from the Civil War. He served as a horse soldier with Grant's Army, and then later he headed up his own special squad," he said.

"I'm afraid we're not familiar with that term, Mr. Post," Glen said.

An amused smile crossed Post's lips. "It's not your father's way to speak of his accomplishments," he said.

"I'd like to know," Glen said. "Both of us would."

"I guess he was younger than you, Jake, when it all started," Post said. "Well, those who were best with a revolver and on a horse were chosen to serve in special squads

23

called horse soldiers. Usually forty men on horseback would ride into enemy territory and raise hell to distract and disorient the rebel army. It was an extremely important and very dangerous job. Your father was a sergeant major until late sixty-two and then was given a field commission to lieutenant. He spent the next three years leading his squad from one town and battle to the next, all across the Deep South."

"He's never spoken of any of that," Glen said. "He hardly ever speaks of the past, except about our mother."

"Like I said, it's not his way to speak of his accomplishments," Post said.

Alice opened the screen door and poked her head out. "One of you boys go fetch your father. Supper is ready," she said.

Dinner was served in the formal dining room where a table large enough to seat twenty was the focal point in the room.

In his spare time, what there was of it, Tillman had built the table, a task that had taken him many years to complete.

Conversation was light and airy and focused mostly on Glen and Jake's daughters, who had many questions about life in the city of Washington.

"You men take coffee on the porch," Alice

said. "I'll call you when dessert is ready."

Tillman, Post, Glen, and Jake took mugs of coffee to the porch and sat in chairs. Tillman stuffed his old, well-used pipe with tobacco and lit it with a wood match.

"I've been studying on something all night. I believe I will go to Laramie to remove the marshal myself," Tillman said.

"Now, Sam, that won't be necessary. I've already told you . . ." Post said.

"I appointed him. It stands to reason I should be the one to remove him from office," Tillman said.

Alice opened the screen door and burst out to the porch. "You'll do no such foolish thing, Sam Tillman," she snapped.

"She's right, Pop. There's no reason you have to go all the way to Laramie when others can do what needs to be done," Glen said.

Tillman quietly puffed on his pipe for a moment. "Others didn't appoint the man. I did. I've never asked others to fix a problem I created. Besides, I already planned to do it before you showed up, Mr. Post," he said.

"Pop, you're going to be sixty-one years old this fall. Listen to reason. Listen to Mr. Post," Glen said.

Tillman looked at Post. "Ten days is what

I ask," he said.

Post raised an eyebrow. "Ten days?"

"You said yourself they wouldn't be arriving with the new man for a week. What's another three extra days?" Tillman said. "That's what I'm asking for."

"Sam, listen to your boys. And Alice," Post said.

Tillman blew smoke and looked at Post. "My mind is made up, and you can't stop me," he said. He looked at Glen and Jake. "And neither can you."

"Go on then. Get yourself killed, you damn old fool," Alice snarled. Then she entered the house and slammed the screen door.

"She's mad as a wet hen," Jake said.

"And then some," Glen said.

"Well, dessert is on the table. Let's go get us some. Then I'll go pack my gear for the morning," Tillman said.

CHAPTER FOUR

Alone in his room, Tillman sat at his desk, fieldstripped his black ivory-handled Colt revolver, and then cleaned it thoroughly. An oil lantern on the desk burned with the flame on high for maximum light. He quietly smoked his pipe as he worked.

Once the Colt was cleaned and oiled, he loaded it with fresh ammunition and then added eighteen rounds to the slots on the sides and rear of the holster belt.

From his gun safe he added a box of one hundred rounds of ammunition to his saddlebags. He also added a box of ammunition for his Model 1894 Winchester rifle into the bags. On the inside of his holster was a small pocket he had made to fit a two-shot, .45 caliber derringer.

He cleaned the derringer, loaded it, and placed it into the pocket. From the desk he picked up his marshal's badge. He held it to the light of the oil lantern on the table.

He used a buffing cloth to polish the badge until it shone brightly in the light from the oil lamp. Gently, almost with reverence, Tillman set the badge on the desk.

After ten in the evening, Post, Glen, and Jake sat in chairs on the porch. Each had a small glass of whiskey. Post smoked a cigar. A wall-mounted oil lamp provided flickering light.

"It's a beautiful spring night, boys," Post said. "The kind made for sleeping with the window open."

Glen took a small sip of his whiskey. "Mr. Post, are you going to stop our father or do we?" he said.

Post blew a cloud of smoke and then grinned. "Do you think the two of you together can stop Sam Tillman?" he said.

"Even if we snuck up on him in the dark and hit him on the head with a fry pan, he'd whip the both of us like children. We know that," Jake said.

"Then how do you plan on stopping him?" Post said.

"We figured you might have some ideas about that," Glen said.

Post chuckled softly. "Apparently you don't know who or what your father is," he said.

"Tell us then," Jake said.

Post puffed on his cigar as he thought. "Do you know how your father became a marshal?" he said.

"Like I said, he never speaks of such things," Glen said.

"After the war, he went to work for the Union Pacific Railroad as it expanded west, as the head of the railroad police. From Nebraska to Utah, your father fought Apaches, Cheyenne, robbers, and every other damn thing with just a handful of men. When they drove in the 'Golden Spike,' he was there keeping the peace," Post said. "When the two railroads took the first passengers for a ride in May of sixty-nine, the federal marshals came calling and offered him a position as United States Marshal."

"We never heard any of that before," Glen said.

Post grinned and tossed back his drink. "So how are you going to accomplish what hundreds before you have tried?" he said. "And failed miserably."

"We'll sleep on it and talk again after breakfast," Glen said.

Tillman awoke at his usual time of five-thirty in the morning. He set a pan of water on the woodstove in his room to heat up, then washed and shaved.

He dressed, packed his gear and saddlebags, and then headed downstairs to breakfast.

Glen, Jake, and Post were already at the table, where Alice was dishing out scrambled eggs, bacon, potatoes, and toast.

Tillman took the chair next to Post, and Alice filled his coffee cup.

"My sons either came to see me off or to try and stop me. Which will it be?" Tillman said.

"Oh, shut up and eat your breakfast, you damn inconsiderate idiot of a man," Alice said.

Tillman looked at his empty plate. "I would, but I don't have any breakfast to eat," he said.

Alice took Tillman's plate and filled it, then set it down.

"You made enough to feed a small army," Tillman said.

"I've been up since four, you old fool, preparing your supplies for the road," Alice said. "Who else is going to look after you?"

"And don't think I don't appreciate that, baby sister," Tillman said.

Alice took a chair next to Glen. "Eat your breakfast and shut up," she said.

Tillman ate some eggs and grabbed a piece of toast. "Now boys, Mr. Post has a broken axle on his carriage. One of you will have to ride to Miles City and order a new one. Alice, looks like Mr. Post will be your guest for a week or so," he said.

Sipping coffee, Post paused and looked at Tillman. "Now, Sam, there is nothing wrong with my carriage," he said.

Tillman ate a slice of bacon and looked at Post. "There is now. Before I went to bed I took a metal saw to the rear axle and sawed it in two," he said.

Glen and Jake grinned at each other.

"Why would you do that, Sam?" Post said.

"Not that I don't trust you to give me the ten days I asked for, but a little insurance never hurt anybody. Neither did a little hard work. You don't mind a little fence-digging to pay for your meals while you're Alice's houseguest, do you, Marshal Post?" Tillman said.

"You had no call to do that, Sam. We've known each other far too long for you to deem me untrustworthy," Post said.

"It ain't a matter of trust. I'm just thinking of how lonely my little sister gets when I'm away from home," Tillman said.

Alice glared at Tillman.

"You don't mind a little company in my

31

absence, do you, baby sister?" Tillman said.

Glen and Jake had to look away to keep themselves from laughing.

"And I'm sure my boys could use an extra hand with the work while I'm away, right, boys?" Tillman said.

"Sure, Pop," Jake said.

Glen looked at Post. "We'll keep him busy enough, Pop," he said. "Don't you worry none."

Post looked at Tillman and sighed.

"Men are all fools," Alice said and stood up.

"Where are you going, baby sister?" Tillman said.

"To get the supplies I prepared for you, you buffoon," Alice said and stormed off to the kitchen.

"I've never seen her so mad," Jake said.

"It's a good thing she doesn't know how to shoot," Glen said.

"Of course, she knows how to shoot," Tillman said as he ate some eggs. "I taught her myself when we were just kids back in the Big Woods of Wisconsin."

CHAPTER FIVE

On the porch, Tillman shook hands with Post, Jake, and Glen and kissed Alice on the cheek.

"Boys, do your best to entertain Mr. Post in my absence. Judging from his nice, soft handshake, he could use some toughening up. Unless Mr. Post wants to walk thirty miles in the sun to escape his chores," Tillman said.

"I fancy not," Post said.

Tillman stepped down off the porch and mounted the saddle.

"Still a horse soldier, aren't you, Sam?" Post said.

Tillman rubbed Blue's neck. "He's going on eighteen, and he's not close to being done yet," he said.

"Hey, Sam, why ten days? You can make it to Laramie in less than five on horseback," Post said. "Two by railroad."

"Let's just say I'd like to stop and see

some old friends along the way," Tillman said and tugged the reins and rode away.

Post dug holes with Glen and Jake for several hours, until he finally had to grab his canteen and sit in the shade of a large tree.

"I'm not as young as I once was, boys," he said. "That's for sure."

Glen and Jake removed their canteens from the wagon and sat beside Post.

"Might as well rest a spell. Aunt Alice will be along with lunch soon," Glen said.

"Mr. Post, what did my father mean when he said he'd like to see some old friends along the way?" Jake said.

Post frowned as he looked at Glen. "Do you want to tell him or should I?" he said.

"Tell me what?" Jake said.

"Those old friends pop wants to see," Glen said. "Pop wants to say his goodbyes."

Tillman rode twenty miles before making camp at dusk. He built a fire and then tended to his horse. Old Blue was nearly eighteen years old now and, at sixteen hundred pounds, a massive and powerful beast. Tillman gave him a good brushing while Blue ate oats. Tillman didn't hobble him; he knew Blue wouldn't wander off during the night in search of sweet grass. There was plenty of the stuff all around them for him to munch on if he got hungry.

"Rode twenty-plus miles today, Blue. We'll make town tomorrow noon," Tillman said. "No sense pushing you or my sixty-year-old back."

Blue turned his massive neck, looked at Tillman, and snorted.

Had there been a need, Blue could have done thirty or more miles before sunset, but there was no need for Tillman to push his old friend so hard.

"Now, let's see what baby sister packed for supper," Tillman said when he was done brushing Blue.

Alice packed just enough food for the trip to Miles City. A steak dusted with salt and pepper and wrapped in waxed paper. Beans and hard crusty bread, coffee. For breakfast there were four eggs, a half pound of bacon, and cornbread. There were a dozen corn dodgers and six large sticks of jerky for saddle snacking.

Alice also filled his eight-ounce silver flask with Tennessee sipping whiskey.

After he ate supper, Tillman spread out his bedroll and used the saddle as a backrest. He lit his pipe, sipped some whiskey, and watched the Montana stars come out for the night.

It was odd how the stars always brought his mind to his wife, Mary Elizabeth. They were sweethearts before the war, and he insisted on marrying her before he left to report to Grant's Army in New York. They didn't see one another again until the end of the war. Years later, she confessed to him that when he rode away to join Grant's Army she never expected to see him again.

He never told her, although he wished he had, that there were times when he would look at her and feel as if he couldn't breathe, he was so overwhelmed with love for her.

He thought she knew it anyway, but he still should have said it more often. Women like to hear things said, even when they knew those things in their hearts.

In seventy, while he was a marshal in Colorado, she gave birth to Glen, so named for his friend Glen Post, who served with him during the war as a scout and spotter. In seventy-one, Jake was born.

In the spring of seventy-nine, while he was still assigned to Colorado, Mary Elizabeth began to cough.

At first the syrup the town doctor gave her seemed to quiet down the cough, but after a while, the cough grew progressively worse.

One night, she woke up in a fit of coughing and spat up blood.

During the war and in his duties with the railroad and as US Marshal, Tillman had seen enough blood to fill a small pond, but the sight of Mary Elizabeth coughing up blood frightened him down to his very soul.

As he sipped whiskey from the flask, memories in his mind were as thick as summer flies.

The night Glen was born, and seeing Mary Elizabeth holding the hours-old baby in her arms, was as fresh as if it happened yesterday.

Sitting in a rocking chair with Glen asleep in his lap while the doctor delivered Jake. At the sound of Jake crying, Glen woke up, and Tillman told him he had a baby brother or sister. Not impressed, Glen fell back asleep.

Holding Mary Elizabeth's hand during her final moments. Her parting words were that she loved him and to please watch over their sons.

He had done his best to live up to those words.

Tillman wiped a tear from his eye and held the flask up to the stars.

"To the very good days of long ago," he said and took a sip.

Post sat in a chair on the porch and drank coffee and smoked a cigar by the light of the wall-mounted lantern. He looked at the millions of stars overhead and wondered when last he saw so many in the night sky.

The nighttime lights in Washington obscured the night sky so that very few stars were visible.

The screen door suddenly opened, and Alice came out and sat next to him.

"Alice, what are you doing still awake?" Post said.

"Couldn't sleep. Mind if I sit awhile with you?" Alice said.

"Please. My cigar bother you?" Post said.

"I've put up with Sam's pipe half my life. Your cigar doesn't bother me," Alice said.

"Sam's boys are fine men," Post said.

"They are that," Alice said. "Mr. Post, you knew Sam would ride out alone, didn't you?"

"I suspected as much," Post said. "I've known him too long not to anticipate his thinking."

"Why couldn't you have just sent your men to Laramie without informing him?" Alice said.

"It doesn't work that way, I'm afraid," Post said. "I fully intended to ride with him to Miles City and meet up with six deputies before reaching Laramie. I never expected him to pull a stunt like he did."

"Why don't you take a horse and ride over to Miles City before it's too late?" Alice asked.

"His boys took every horse from the barn, including mine, and took them to their own places," Post said. "I can't exactly go steal one in the dead of night, now can I? And I don't fancy a thirty-mile walk on a dusty road to Miles City."

Alice sighed. "Damn my hardheaded brother," she said.

Post grinned. "He has a way about him, doesn't he?"

"How are your hands?"

"Sore. Red," Post said. "It's been a while since I've labored such."

"Be grateful Sam isn't working you," Alice said.

Post grinned. "Got any liniment?"

"Around here? A closet full," Alice said.

Miles City was a bustling town of two thousand residents, mostly due to the two army forts established after the Battle of Little Bighorn. One of the forts was named

Fort Keogh after Captain Myles Keogh, who died at that battle.

Tillman sold many a head of cattle to the army to feed the hundreds of soldiers stationed at the two forts.

It was a warm, airless morning that spoke of a hot summer ahead when Tillman rode Blue along Main Street. He dismounted in front of the sheriff's office.

"I won't be long," he told Blue with a scratch to his ears.

Sheriff Dan Woodson was behind his desk when Tillman entered the office.

"Sam, what brings you to town?" Woodson asked.

"Lunch. Had yours?" Tillman said.

"So, Sam, where are you off to so close to retirement?" Woodson asked.

They were in the restaurant located in the lobby of the Hotel Miles.

"My last official bit of business," Tillman said as he sliced into his steak.

"Well, if you get tired of retirement, I could always use a good deputy in town," Woodson said.

"Full-time rancher starting in thirty days, but thanks for the offer," Tillman said. "Dan, I need a favor."

"Sure, Sam."

Tillman removed a sealed envelope from his vest pocket and set it on the table. "Hold this for me until I get back," Tillman said. "If I don't make it back, give it to my sister, Alice."

Woodson looked at Tillman.

"No questions, Dan," Tillman said.

Woodson knew better than to ask any, nodded, and reached for the envelope.

"Obliged," Tillman said.

Tillman took a walk around town after lunch. The streets were clogged with people and wagons. If men still rode on horseback, the evidence wasn't visible in Miles City.

It wasn't so long ago that Miles City was all muddy streets with just a few buildings and a tent saloon.

Now half the buildings had electric lights and indoor plumbing.

Talk was that in five years, a telephone exchange would be approved by the town council, although Tillman believed people talked too much already as it was.

He stopped into the First Bank of Miles City and withdrew one thousand dollars for traveling money.

At the general store, he stopped to pick up a few things, and then he walked Blue to the railroad station.

For once, the four-o'clock train was on time. With Blue in the boxcar, Tillman sat in a middle car and watched the scenery roll by as the train traveled south to Deadwood, South Dakota.

The train was scheduled to arrive in Deadwood at midnight. There was nothing to do on the ride except read newspapers, nap, and watch the countryside roll by until it was too dark to see anything.

The riding car was warm, and he placed his head against the window and closed his eyes.

1863, The Deep South

Wearing the uniform of a second lieutenant, Tillman sat atop a tall, powerful horse. He had just led a charge on Confederate soldiers caught off guard at their small, riverside encampment.

A Confederate soldier broke ranks and ran toward the woods.

Tillman gave chase on his horse.

The Confederate soldier ran into the woodlands with Tillman not far behind. The Confederate soldier ran and ran. Downhill and across a stream, and still Tillman kept coming. Exhausted, the Confederate soldier fell to the ground, gasping for breath.

Tillman rode up to the fallen Confederate

soldier. He held a massive Colt Dragoon pistol in his right hand.

The Confederate soldier got on his knees. Tillman cocked the Colt and aimed it at the Confederate soldier. They made eye contact. The Confederate soldier was little more than a boy in uniform.

The Confederate soldier knew he was about to die and closed his eyes. Seconds ticked off, and when the Confederate soldier opened his eyes, Tillman was gone.

1901

Tillman must have fallen asleep, because the sudden jerk of the train coming to a full stop took him by surprise, and he nearly hit his head on the seat in front of him.

Just a handful of people got off the train with him. Spread out over four square miles, Deadwood boasted a population of thirty-five-hundred residents. Gone were the days of Wild Bill Hickok, Seth Bullock, and the early lawlessness that had infected the town. Much had changed in twenty-five years.

The Nuttal and Mann's Saloon, where Hickok was murdered, burned down in seventy-nine, and had since been rebuilt. A clothing store took its place and then, finally, a beer hall. Another amazing thing about Deadwood was the mayor had purchased an electric generator from the Edison Company in New Jersey, and the town boasted of having fifteen electric light bulbs illuminating the center of town. Everything else was lit by oil lamps or candles.

As he led Blue along Main Street, Tillman paused at the sheriff's office.

A lamp was lit, and someone was at the desk.

Tillman entered the office, and a sleepy-eyed deputy sat up straight.

"The good folks of Deadwood are paying for protection, and here you are sleeping on the job," Tillman said.

"Can I help you with something?" the deputy said.

"I'm United States Marshal Sam Tillman," Tillman said.

The deputy leaned forward and turned up the flame on the oil lamp. "Gosh, it *is* you," he said.

"Did you just use the word 'gosh'?" Tillman said.

"Sorry. It ain't often we get so famous a lawman in this town anymore," the deputy said.

"Are you the only deputy on duty?" Tillman said.

"Me and another. He's on patrol," the

deputy said.

"What's a good hotel I can stay at that hasn't been torn or burned down?" Tillman said. "And by good, I mean no bedbugs."

"Try the Deadwood Inn," the deputy said. "It's right on Main Street, and they have a livery for your horse."

"Obliged," Tillman said.

Tillman left the office, and the deputy stood up from his desk and went to the window.

"Sam Tillman. Son of a bitch," the deputy said.

Tillman found the Deadwood Inn a few blocks away from the sheriff's office. It was four stories high with balconies on the top two floors. Tillman brought his saddlebags with him when he entered the lobby and registered. The room was seven dollars for one night. He paid two dollars extra to have Blue stabled and fed.

Tillman's room was on the fourth floor facing the street. A wall-mounted oil lamp was already lit when he entered the room. Not yet tired, he dug out his flask and added two ounces of whiskey to the water glass on the desk and then added water from the pitcher.

Then he stuffed his pipe with fresh tobacco and sat on the balcony to sip his drink and watch the quiet, dark street below.

In the distance, the electric lights of the town square were visible.

Being in Deadwood naturally brought to mind Wild Bill Hickok. He first met the man in August of seventy-one. Tillman, a deputy back then, was sent with five other deputies to Abilene, Kansas, to arrest the outlaw John Wesley Hardin. Hickok was elected town marshal, one of many law enforcement positions the man held in his short life. Hardin was hiding under the name Wesley Clemmons. Hickok didn't know Hardin was in town, and the outlaw escaped before he could be arrested.

Hickok later told Tillman that Hardin was a likable young fellow who broke no laws while in town and gave Hickok no cause to arrest him.

Hickok proved to be everything Tillman heard or read about the man. As tall as Tillman, with hair past his shoulders, he wore two 1851 Navy Colt revolvers in a reverse twist, or cavalry draw, in a sash around his waist. Tillman was very familiar with the cavalry draw, having worn the backwards flap-holster during the war.

Five years later, as a full federal marshal, Tillman and two deputies rode to Deadwood at the request of the territorial governor to try and establish law and order in the famously lawless town.

They arrived a week after Hickok was killed by Jack McCall, who shot Hickok in the back of the head at point-blank range.

When they rode into town, a funeral procession was taking place on Main Street. Tillman approached a woman dressed in black, who was at the front of the procession.

"What happened here?" Tillman asked her.

"They shot him," the woman said. "The coward Jack McCall done shot my Bill."

Soon after, Seth Bullock arrived and was elected town marshal.

Tillman lifted his drink to the street below.

"To the very good days of long ago," he said.

CHAPTER SIX

Tillman was eating breakfast in the hotel café when Sheriff Tom Pullman joined him at the table. Awake at five-thirty, Tillman requested a bath and a shave. He entered the café at seven, when it opened for business.

"My deputy said Sam Tillman was in town, and I had to see for myself," Pullman said. "I'm Tom Pullman, Sheriff of Deadwood."

"Nice to meet you, Sheriff," Tillman said. "Have some coffee with me?"

"Believe I will," Pullman said.

A waitress brought a cup to Pullman and filled it.

"So what brings you to town?" Pullman asked.

"Old friends," Tillman said.

Pullman sipped his coffee and slowly nodded. "So you're not here in any official capacity," he said.

"My business is elsewhere," Tillman said. "But I thought I'd pay a visit to an old friend and some ghosts on the way."

Pullman nodded. "I reckon you'd know quite a bit about both," he said.

"Much has changed since those days," Tillman said.

"Some folks say Deadwood has become civilized," Pullman said.

"That's a fancy was of saying all the fun has gone out of a town," Tillman said.

Pullman grinned as he took a sip of coffee. "Maybe so, but people seem to live longer these days," he said. "Of course, I'm not so sure that's a good thing, either."

Before leaving Deadwood, Tillman purchased four bottles of bourbon whiskey at the general store on Main Street, along with a sack of food supplies that included ten pounds of beans, bacon, flour, coffee, and sugar.

"And let me get a pouch of tobacco and rolling papers," he told the clerk. "The best you got."

As he loaded the supplies onto Blue's saddle outside the store, Tillman noticed people on the street staring at him.

The clerk from the store came out with a

small paper sack. "You forgot your tobacco," he said.

"Obliged," Tillman said. "Funny, but I remember the people of this town as being a bit friendlier."

"Don't hold it against them, Marshal. It's been years since they've seen a real gunman up close," the clerk said.

"There was a time when that's all they saw," Tillman said and mounted the saddle.

Tillman rode half the day to the hills near the small mining town of Terry. Up a hill, in a clearing, stood a small log cabin. A corral with three horses, a water pump with a bucket, and a small shed accompanied the cabin.

Tillman dismounted at the corral and stood quietly while his eyes scanned the terrain and buildings.

"Jane. Jane Canary, it's Sam Tillman," he shouted. "Show yourself, Jane."

Slowly the door to the shed opened, and the barrel of a shotgun exposed itself.

"No need for that scattergun, Jane," Tillman said.

"Is that really you, Sam Tillman?" Jane said.

"Come out and have a look for yourself," Tillman said.

The door to the shed opened and Jane

slowly walked out. She looked at Tillman and smiled. "Howdy, Sam," she said.

"Howdy, Jane," Tillman said.

"You're a long way from Miles City," Jane said.

"A fair piece."

"Bring me some sipping whiskey?"

"Four bottles."

"Had yer lunch yet?"

"No, Jane, I have not," Tillman said.

"Care to join me?"

"Depends on what you're cooking."

"Got a rabbit stew in the pot," Jane said. "Why don't we get started on one of those bottles you brung while it cooks."

The interior of Jane's cabin was rustic and basic with a table, bed, woodstove, fireplace, and some cabinets.

Jane and Tillman sat at the table with bowls of rabbit stew and hard bread for dipping.

"Excellent stew, Jane," Tillman said.

Jane held a bottle of bourbon to her lips and swallowed several ounces in one large gulp. She set the bottle on the table and wiped her lips on her sleeve.

"Jane, there's no call to drink like that," Tillman said.

"No call not to, neither," Jane said. "Least

you got the good sense not to call me Calamity. I'd a shot you if you had, old friend or not."

"I heard you joined up with Buffalo Bill's Wild West show for a spell," Tillman said. "How is the old pip-squeak?"

"Short as ever, only now he hides his big belly wearing a woman's girdle and a wig to hide his bald spot," Jane said and laughed.

Tillman chuckled. "Doesn't surprise me none," he said. "Old Cody always was a man concerned about his vanity, to be sure."

"They asked me to go to Buffalo in New York, for the world's fair event. The President is going to be there. I ain't said yes as yet."

"You should go, Jane," Tillman said. "Get away from this old cabin for a while and mix with some people."

"I'm studying on it," Jane said. "My eyes ain't what they once were. I'm afraid I might miss and kill a bystander. That's why I'm carrying a scattergun."

"Time gets to us all, I'm afraid," Tillman said.

"Even you, Sam?"

"I need spectacles to read the newspaper these days," Tillman said.

Jane chuckled. "Good thing I ain't got no newspapers then," she said.

"How did you like New York City?"

"A worse smelling place I never been," Jane said. "The whole city smells like a giant outhouse in July. I did see me a few of those horseless carriages on the streets. Stink of oil and black smoke. Nasty things, they are. Noisy, too."

Jane picked up the bottle and took another drink. "And rats the size of puppies everywhere in the streets," she said. "Disgusting place better suited to the rats than people. And birds on the rooftops in cages."

"Cages?"

"People keep them as pets," Jane said. "They let them loose to fly around, and they shit on everything."

"Well, I've seen rats and I've seen birds, but I've never seen a horseless carriage," Tillman said. "I hope to, though."

"They say in ten years, they will replace the horse," Jane said.

"I doubt that," Tillman said. "But nothing surprises me anymore."

"I did see me a flicker show in the Longacre Square in Manhattan," Jane said. "You put a nickel in and turn a handle, and it shows a scene of something or another. The one I saw, a woman took off all her clothes. I don't think it was meant for women to see. It's very popular. Men with pockets full of nickels lined up out the door."

Jane took another long swallow from the bottle. "I never did thank you for bringing that murderous scum Jack McCall to trial in Yankton. Too bad they couldn't hang the bastard twice for murdering my Bill."

"It was a long time ago, Jane," Tillman said. "Best forgotten."

"I ain't been to town for supplies in a month," Jane said. "Did you bring me some rolling tobacco and paper?"

"And flour, coffee, beans, bacon, sugar, bread, and a few other things."

"For a man with so hard a bark, you always had a kind streak in you, Sam," Jane said. "A lot like my Bill in that regard. If he hadn't felt sorry for that coward McCall and given him money for breakfast after besting him at cards, the coward wouldn't have felt resentment toward my Bill and shot him in the head. I know, Sam. I was there."

"Like I said, Jane, it was a long time ago," Tillman said. "Some memories are best left to rest."

Jane gulped some more whiskey and then said, "What brings you here anyway?"

"Headed south on assignment," Tillman said. "Just thought I'd make a quick stop to say hello."

"Stay the night?"

"Got a train to catch at ten tonight," Tillman said.

Jane nodded and took another swallow from the bottle. "Is it true what I heard, that a long time ago you was with the Rangers that captured old Wesley Hardin down in the Panhandle?"

"I was there, but I didn't do much," Tillman said. "It was all the Rangers doing."

Jane opened the tobacco pouch Tillman had brought her and rolled a cigarette. Tillman struck a match and lit it for her.

"I heard Hardin caught his pistol on his suspenders and couldn't draw down on them," Jane said.

"Old John Hardin was something all right," Tillman said.

"I heard years later from an old Ranger that Hardin was scared to draw down on you, so he gave up peaceable," Jane said.

Tillman shrugged. "People talk. Let me get them supplies for you, Jane. I need to be on my way."

Tillman stepped outside and removed the large sack from the saddle. He paused to look around for a moment. It bothered him a bit that so well known a woman as Jane

Canary was a forgotten piece of ancient history.

For a time Jane's face was on every dime novel across the country, her guns blazing beside a doctored-up drawing of Bill Hickok or some other known outlaw. Seeing her living in such squalor spoke of the fleeting taste of the general public when it came to their heroes.

He stuck a hundred dollars into the bag of coffee, and then brought the sack into the cabin and set it on the table.

"The coffee is ready, Sam. Would you have a cup with me?" Jane said.

"Sure," Tillman said.

Jane filled two cups with thick black coffee, then sat and rolled another cigarette.

Tillman filled his pipe, lit it, and then Jane's cigarette.

"I always made good coffee," Jane said. "I learned to make it strong for Bill after he woke with a hangover from a Chinese pipe. When his eyes took to hurting, he said the Chinese pipe eased the pain."

Tillman sipped his coffee. "Good and strong and hot," he said. "Like my mother used to make."

"You always were a kind man, Sam," Jane said. "Back in my famous days, you were the only man I can remember who didn't try to take advantage of my womanhood when I was drunk. You always were respectful, which is something I truly admire."

"I heard you married," Tillman said.

"Rancher named Clinton Burke," Jane said. "Had me a daughter, but circumstances being what they was at the time, I gave her up for adoption. Old Clinton passed years ago, I'm afraid. She'd be about fourteen, I guess."

"Jane, maybe I'll stop back on my way home, but right now I have a train to catch," Tillman said.

Jane hugged Tillman tightly before he mounted his horse.

"Don't go get yourself kilt, Sam," Jane said. "I ain't got too many friends left from the old days."

"I'll do my best to stay alive, Jane," Tillman said.

"Sam, do you ever feel like things are closing in on you? Like everything we knew is all gone and not coming back?" Jane said.

"Oftentimes I do, Jane," Tillman said and mounted Blue. "But there's nothing you can do but roll with the punches. You take care of yourself, Calamity Jane."

Jane grinned as she watched Tillman settle himself in the saddle.

"I should shoot you for that, Sam Tillman," Jane said.

Tillman touched the rim of his hat, turned Blue, and rode away.

Jane watched as Tillman rode down the hill. She smiled until he was out of view, then her face saddened and she returned to the cabin.

CHAPTER SEVEN

As he rode back to Deadwood to catch the train, Tillman thought about Jane Canary. It struck him odd how millions knew the name Calamity Jane, but no one knew the name Jane Canary.

In her youth, she was a wild and pretty woman, given to fits of anger and streaks of gentle compassion. She fought Indians, rode with Custer, and held her own with any man, including Hickok. After Hickok's death, she took to hard drinking and let herself go, but still possessed fire in her soul. In 1878, she saved passengers on a stagecoach under attack from several plains Indians. He read in the paper that she was fired from Cody's show for drunkenness and profanity.

She wasn't but forty-seven or -eight years old, but her looks were far gone and she appeared decades older than she was.

He feared she would die alone and forgotten, much like the old west itself.

She was right, though. Things were closing in and changing everything. Those things were called progress.

And there was no stopping progress. You could live in the past, deny progress was coming, or embrace it. The one thing you couldn't do was ignore it. Those who did were left behind in the new world of civilization.

When Tillman reached Deadwood, he purchased a ticket at the railroad station and waited for the train to arrive.

He sat on a bench at the end of the platform and tethered Blue to the hitching post. He reached into his satchel, removed a twenty-year-old dime novel, and looked at the cover. *The Life and Adventures of Calamity Jane,* the cover read. An artist's drawing depicted Jane in her prime, dressed in dungarees with a blue shirt, firing two silver Colt revolvers, one boot on a man's back.

Tillman put on his reading glasses, flipped pages, and started to read. "You're right about one thing, Jane," he said. "It's never coming back."

As Blue alerted him to the advancing train, he put the book away and waited for the train to arrive.

After housing Blue in the boxcar, Tillman

entered the train and took a window seat. After the train left the platform, a conductor came by to punch Tillman's ticket.

"If I'm asleep later when we reach Omaha, give me a gentle nudge," Tillman said.

"Certainly," the conductor said.

"And what time does the dining car open?" Tillman said.

"Ten minutes after we leave the station," the conductor said.

"Obliged," Tillman said.

As he drank a cup of coffee in the dining car, Tillman flipped pages in a newspaper he picked up at the railroad station.

At a table against the wall, a man dressed in a suit sipped coffee and studied Tillman.

Tillman stuffed his pipe and lit it with a wood match. He flipped pages in the newspaper to the back and scanned the sports page.

The man at the table against the wall stood up and walked to Tillman's table.

"Excuse me. My name is James Brass. Are you Marshal Sam Tillman, by any chance?" he said.

Tillman looked up at Brass. "I am. Why are you asking?" Tillman said.

"I'm a reporter with the *New York Register.* I covered the death and funeral of John

61

Hardin back in ninety-five. I was wondering if I may sit and talk with you for a bit," Brass said.

"Talk about what?" Tillman said.

"May I sit?" Brass said.

Tillman nodded, and Brass took the chair opposite Tillman.

"I spoke with a few of the retired Texas Rangers who arrested Hardin in Florida. They told me Hardin surrendered so peacefully only because he was afraid of you. Is that true, as they told me?" Brass said.

"Do you want it to be true?" Tillman said.

"I'm afraid I don't understand," Brass said.

"I'm a United States Marshal, son," Tillman said. "If you're looking for a story, try Mark Twain or Stephen Crane. I hear they're good at writing stories."

"But, Marshal . . ."

Tillman stood up. "Have a good evening," he said and left the dining car.

In his seat, Tillman lit his pipe and looked out the window at the darkness. "Newspaper reporter," he said aloud. "God help me."

1877, Florida
It was August of 1877 when Tillman and

six Texas Rangers traveled to Florida to arrest John Wesley Hardin for murder.

As Hardin was wanted by the federal government as well as the state of Texas, Tillman was sent by Washington to assist the Rangers with Hardin's capture.

The heat was practically unbearable, as were the mosquitoes, brought out by the morning rain showers. Tillman and the other men met the sheriff's department in Pensacola, where Hardin was supposedly in hiding.

Pensacola was a seaport near the Alabama border, and everything smelled of salt and seaweed at low tide. It got in your nose and stayed there like a bad cold.

Hiding under the name of James Swain, Hardin did anything but keep a low profile for a man wanted by Texas and the federal government. However, locals claimed no knowledge of Hardin's whereabouts, and it took days of searching before they discovered his hideout after a local gave it away for a twenty-dollar gold piece.

Early one August morning, Tillman, the Texas Rangers, and a team of Pensacola deputies rode into a railroad stockyard and dismounted fifty feet from an abandoned boxcar.

"We know you're in there, Hardin. Throw

out your guns and come out peaceably or we . . ." a Ranger shouted.

"You go to hell," Hardin shouted from inside the boxcar.

"We know you're not alone, John. We don't want to have to kill anybody. Surrender, and there won't be any shooting," the Ranger said.

"Screw you, Ranger," Hardin shouted.

"Our warrant is just for you, John," the Ranger said. "Your friends don't have to get hurt if they'll —"

"This ain't my friends, Ranger. It's your mama and sister in here with me," Hardin said. "They give you their regards and ask for another bottle to keep the party going."

Standing beside his tall horse, Tillman shouted, "Enough of this crap, Hardin. Come out or I come in. If I come in, you and your friends are dead men. I promise you that much."

"Who's the big mouth doing the talking?" Hardin shouted.

"United States Marshal Sam Tillman," Tillman shouted.

For several seconds everything went still. Then the door to the boxcar slid open.

"All right, Hardin, come out with your hands . . ." a Ranger said.

A man jumped from the boxcar with a

Colt revolver in his hand. As he hit the ground he cocked the hammer.

Without hesitation, Tillman drew his Colt, cocked it and shot the man once in the chest, and then walked up to him and kicked the gun out of his hand.

The man was still alive, but not for much longer.

"Why did you do a fool thing like that?" Tillman said. "Didn't you hear the Ranger say the warrant was just for Hardin? Stupid isn't much of a talent, son. Neither is being dead."

"You kilt me," the man said, looking up at Tillman.

"I am sorry about that, but I couldn't chance you killing one of us," Tillman said.

"I'm kilt, you bastard," the man said.

"Nothing I can do about it, son. Best make your peace with your maker while you still got breath," Tillman said.

"Screw him, too," the man said and closed his eyes.

Tillman sighed and then looked at the boxcar. "You got this man killed for no reason, Hardin," he said. "He's not even wanted, you son of a bitch."

"You go to hell," Hardin said.

"You first," Tillman said. He emptied his Colt into the boxcar and then calmly reloaded and emptied it again.

As he reloaded a second time, Tillman said, "I can do this all day and night, Hardin. Can you?"

There were a few moments of silence.

"What's your offer?" Hardin said.

"Your life," Tillman said. "You'll do a stretch, but you'll be alive."

"Hold your fire, Tillman," Hardin said. "I give up."

"Toss out your guns," Tillman said. "All of them."

Several revolvers flew out the open boxcar door.

Tillman turned and looked back at the Rangers and deputies. "Well, go get him," he said.

As the Rangers and deputies approached the boxcar, Tillman walked to his horse, mounted the saddle, and simply rode away.

1901

Tillman opened his eyes when the conductor gently shook him on the shoulder.

"Excuse me, Marshal, but the stop is Omaha," the conductor said.

"Thank you," Tillman said. "I'll need a few minutes to get my horse from the boxcar."

"We have a one-hour layover. Take your

time," the conductor said.

Tillman stood and stretched.

"Oh, my sixty-year-old back," he said.

As the train stopped, Brass stood up from his seat at the end of the car and then followed Tillman as he walked out to the platform.

CHAPTER EIGHT

Tillman spent a restless night in a bed too soft to suit him at the Hotel Omaha. Before breakfast he requested a bath and then shaved, dressed, and took breakfast in the hotel dining room.

He lingered for a while over coffee and an Omaha newspaper.

He left the hotel a few minutes before ten and walked along Main Street. A few seconds later, Brass exited the hotel and followed Tillman. At the street corner, Tillman paused to light his pipe.

Omaha was an enormous town of one hundred thousand residents, and was one of the most prominent cities in the country. Its rise to prominence actually began in eighteen sixty-two, when it was chosen as the site for westward expansion of the railroad to begin. When construction began in sixty-six after the war, thousands flocked to town searching for jobs.

Once the railroad expansion was complete, the famous Omaha stockyards quickly followed, and the city became a hub of commerce. Electric light bulbs were everywhere. So were telephone lines. It was a warm spring morning, and women were dressed in high-fashioned and tight-looking shoes. They all looked uncomfortable in the heat. Men wore fine suits and looked equally as uncomfortable in their ties.

To Tillman, it seemed fashion and comfort didn't go hand in hand in these modern times.

Few horses were on the streets, as carriages dominated the mode of transportation. Guns weren't banned, but no one wore one out in the open. Tillman drew looks from people he passed on the street as his Colt sidearm was clearly visible, as was his badge.

Behind Tillman, Brass kept a safe distance.

There were many fine shops and stores on Main Street, but in the background, the aroma of the stockyards wafted in the slight breeze. Tillman passed a restaurant that had tables on the street where people were eating breakfast.

Why a person would want to eat breakfast on the sidewalk where the air smelled of horse manure and cattle was a mystery to

Tillman, but the people eating didn't seem to notice or mind.

As he neared the Omaha Opera House, a banner stretched across the wide street. *World Heavyweight Boxing Champion James J. Jeffries Exhibition Tour,* the banner read.

At the opera house, a stand-up street sign read, *Boxing Exhibition ten to two today only.*

Tillman paused to read the sign and look at the photographs of Jeffries in action. Jeffries was a large, muscular man who dominated the world of boxing.

Tillman entered the very crowded lobby where people were lined up to purchase tickets for the boxing exhibition. Several ushers kept the crowd under control and moved the line along.

An usher supervising the ropes spotted Tillman and approached him.

"I'm sorry, sir, but firearms aren't permitted inside the opera house," the usher said.

Tillman moved his jacket slightly to expose his badge.

"Apologies, Marshal. Is there something I can help you with?" the usher said.

"The boxing exhibition, which hall is it being held in?" Tillman said.

"The main hall, but you need to buy a

ticket. I'm afraid it's sold out," the usher said.

Tillman stared at the usher.

"I suppose we can make an exception for the law. Follow me, Marshal," the usher said.

Tillman followed the usher along a hallway to the large entrance doors of the main theatre. He opened the door and Tillman entered. The theatre was lavish, with electric lights and red carpets.

The seating capacity was one thousand, and every seat was filled. A boxing ring had been constructed on the stage. James Jeffries skipped rope in the center of the ring.

Sports reporters were lined up at a table, some with typewriters. Tillman walked to the two reporters in the center and quietly leaned close and flicked the ear of the man in front of him.

The man jumped to his feet, spun around, and snarled, "You son of a bitch, what do you —"

"Howdy, Wyatt," Tillman said.

Wyatt Earp's anger immediately faded. He touched the shoulder of Bat Masterson and said, "Hey, Bat, look what the cat dragged in."

Masterson stood, turned, and looked at Tillman.

"Looks like they let anybody wear a badge these days, Wyatt," Masterson said.

"Even grandpas," Earp said.

"Can this grandpa interest you gentlemen in a cup of coffee?" Tillman said.

"I don't know about the gentlemen part, but I can use one," Earp said.

Earp and Masterson grabbed their jackets, and the three men exited the hall to the lobby and then the street.

As they walked along the sidewalk, Brass, who was seated on a bench in a small park across the street, stood and followed them from a safe distance.

Chapter Nine

1901, Omaha

"The last time I saw you was at the Fitzsimmons fight in ninety-six, if memory serves me right," Earp said.

After his retirement from law enforcement, Wyatt Earp dipped his hands into many pies, including gold mining in Alaska and refereeing major boxing matches across the country.

The belief by the public and the boxing commission was that Wyatt Earp would never try to fix a fight, and that made him very much in demand.

They were at a small café across the street from the opera house.

"What in God's name are you doing in Omaha?" Masterson said.

"I read the papers, Bat," Tillman said. "Been following your story on Jeffries's cross-country trip on his way to his fight in California. I have some business not far from here and thought I'd stop over and say hello."

For a decade, Masterson was one of the most famous sports reporters in the country, a profession he took up after he retired from law enforcement.

"I swear, why aren't you retired by now?" Masterson asked.

"In three weeks or so, I will be," Tillman said. "Got a nice little spread in Montana. Me and my two boys. What about you, Wyatt? Are you going to referee the fight?"

"They asked me to," Earp said. "I've done about thirty of them now."

"And you knew we'd be in Omaha, Sam?" Masterson said.

"We get the newspapers, even in Montana. I read where you were touring with the champ. I thought I would mix business with pleasure and stop by and say hello," Tillman said.

"Still tracking outlaws, Sam?" Earp said. "It's a young man's game, you know."

"In three weeks or so, I will let the young men have it," Tillman said. "Me and my two boys will spend our days working our spread. What about you, Wyatt? Are you going to keep refereeing fights?"

"That's why I'm here," Earp said. "Bat roped me into touring with him and the champ. After that, we'll see."

"How is your wife?" Tillman asked.

"Josie is fine, just fine," Earp said. "She's in San Francisco, waiting for us. After the fight, we'll head back to Alaska and check our claim. After that, maybe we'll settle in California for a bit."

Tillman took a sip of his coffee. "I still got saddle sores from chasing old Dave Rudabaugh four hundred miles."

"My tailbone was sore for a month after that," Masterson said.

"Tailbone, hell. My ass was sore as if I ran naked through a mesquite bush and sat on it for a week," Earp said.

The three men were silent for a moment, as if reflecting. Tillman struck a match and lit his pipe.

"You know something, Sam? I miss the old days of Dodge City and Tombstone," Earp said.

"I was shot three times in Dodge City and stabbed once," Tillman said.

"I know, but we were young men back then," Earp said.

"Well, I don't miss the outlaws or the years I spent in the saddle chasing them, but getting old is not all it's made out to be for sure," said Masterson.

"I would do it all over again for the chance

to be young one more time," Earp said.

"Haven't you heard, Wyatt, that with age comes wisdom?" Tillman said.

"With age comes a sore ass and bony knees," Earp said.

The three men laughed.

"Still got that big horse I saw you riding in ninety-six?" Earp said.

Tillman nodded. "Old Blue. He's in the hotel livery."

"What do you say, Bat? Let's rent a pair of horses and go for a ride," Earp said. "I'm sick of watching Jeffries skip rope and sweat."

"As long as my saddle comes with a pillow," Masterson said.

"There's a livery a few blocks from here that rents horses and wagons," Earp said. "Sam, meet us there in thirty minutes."

After Earp and Masterson left the café, Tillman lingered for a few minutes to finish his coffee.

At a table behind Tillman, Brass sat with a cup of coffee and his notebook. In the book, he drew a sketch of Tillman, Earp, and Masterson having coffee at the table. He captioned the sketch *Three Legends.*

Brass watched as Tillman left a dollar on the table and walked out to the street.

Tillman held Blue by the reins and smoked his pipe in front of the hotel livery.

He wasn't a man given to sentiment, but talking with Earp and Masterson had brought to the surface many old memories he hadn't thought about in years.

Then, with people watching as if they'd never seen a man on horseback before, Tillman mounted the saddle and rode Blue to the livery where Masterson and Earp waited.

"I swear to God, the people in Omaha have never seen a man ride a horse before," Tillman said.

"They've become civilized, Sam, but don't hold it against them," Masterson said. "Some of them have good qualities."

"Like what?" Earp said.

"Clean silverware and linen napkins," Masterson said.

Masterson mounted the saddle on his rented horse. "This was your idea, Wyatt. Lead the way," he said.

"We'll follow the train tracks out of town," Earp said.

As they rode past the café, Brass was seated in a chair out front, and he immediately drew another sketch.

A few miles east of Omaha, Tillman, Earp, and Masterson dismounted their horses and stood in an open field of wildflowers and tall grass.

"It doesn't take much to escape civilization, does it?" Masterson said.

"Hell, even the wildflowers are civilized around here," Earp said.

They walked the horses to the shade of a tall tree, then sat under it on the soft grass. Blue decided to munch on the grass, and the two rented horses followed his lead.

Tillman filled his pipe and lit it with a wood match.

"That looks like the same pipe you had in ninety-six," Earp said.

"Since seventy-one, when I purchased it at a tobacco shop in Cheyenne," Tillman said. "Before that, I had one that came from England and was hand carved. I traded it to a Cheyenne chief for a horse blanket."

"And that Colt you're wearing, it's the one you wore during the Dodge City Wars, isn't it?" Masterson said.

"A man doesn't give up the finest gun ever made just because it has some years on it," Tillman said.

"Remember Dodge City, Bat?" Earp said.

"Who could forget it?" Masterson said.

"Me and Sam rode in to help you fight off the crooked mayor. What was that, in eighty-three?" Earp said.

"In June, I believe," Tillman said.

"Me on the left side of the street, Bat on the right, and old Sam just rides down the center of the street as easy as you please. But Sam always did have balls of iron, if you ask me," Earp said.

"And a head full of mush to go along with them," Tillman said.

"I never did see a faster draw. Even Doc Holliday would have given pause to draw down on you, Sam," Earp said.

"With age also comes slower reflexes," Tillman said.

Earp looked at the Colt in Tillman's holster. "I wouldn't bet on it," he said.

"Who would like a cup of coffee?" Masterson said.

Masterson produced a pint silver flask from his jacket pocket and tossed it to Tillman. The three men sat in a circle on the ground and Earp dipped into his jacket for his cigar case. He gave Masterson and Tillman a cigar and matches.

Tillman set his pipe aside, and the three men lit their cigars off wood matches.

Each took a sip from the silver flask.

"You know, in all the gunfights I've been in, I never so much as got a scratch," Earp said. "After the O.K. fight, I took seven bullet holes in my duster and hat, and not a one drew blood."

"Twice for me," Masterson said.

"All told, I've been shot six times," Tillman said.

"I guess I'll live out my days never knowing what it's like to get shot," Earp said.

Earp took a sip from the flask and gave it to Masterson.

"Sam, you're heeled. Do Wyatt a favor and shoot him so he can enjoy the experience before he lives out his days," Masterson said and took a sip.

"If he accidentally kills me, who will finish my autobiography?" Earp said.

Masterson gave the flask to Tillman. "I've seen what he's written, Sam. It's pretty much all bullshit," he said.

"Not all of it. I corrected the record about the O.K. Corral actually being in an alleyway and a few other things," Earp said.

"See, Sam? Bullshit," Masterson said. "How about it, Wyatt? Why not give Sam his due and write what really happened in Dodge City?"

"What do you say, Sam? Want me to tell the whole story?" Earp said.

"Don't even consider it," Tillman said. "The last thing I ever want to see is my face on a dime novel."

Masterson looked at Earp. "Hear that, Wyatt?"

"Hey, you've had your share of dime novels, Mr. New York City newspaper man," Earp said.

"Boys, a toast," Tillman said. "To the very good days of long ago."

Tillman sipped and gave the flask to Masterson. "May we live long enough to see them return," he said and sipped.

Earp took the flask. "To the truth! May it never be told," he said.

"Boys, I have a train to catch," Tillman said.

Tillman, Earp, and Masterson rode into Omaha along Main Street as if they owned the entire city. They dismounted in front of Tillman's hotel.

"We'll see you off at the station," Masterson said.

When Tillman entered the lobby of the hotel, Brass hid his face behind a newspaper.

Tillman shook hands with Earp and Masterson before boarding the train.

"Good seeing you boys again," he said.

"I swear, Sam," Earp said.

Tillman took the first step onto the train.

"Hey, Sam," Masterson said. "I got the newspaper byline and Wyatt got the dime novels, but you were the best of the lot."

Tillman grinned. "Maybe I'll come see you boys at the fight," he said.

"You do that, Sam," Earp said. "We'll save a ringside seat for you."

Tillman entered the train and the door closed. A few moments later, the train rolled out of the station.

Masterson and Earp looked at each other.

"I swear, Bat," Earp said.

"Yeah. Let's get back to the opera house," Masterson said. "And watch Jeffries sweat some more."

CHAPTER TEN

Tillman sat by a window in a riding car. He opened a newspaper and began to read when the conductor entered the car to punch tickets.

"Ticket, sir," the conductor said.

Tillman gave him the ticket and the conductor punched it. "Thank you, sir," the conductor said.

"What time does the dining car open?" Tillman said.

"Eight."

"Obliged," Sam said.

The conductor moved along. In the last seat in the car, he stopped by Brass. "Ticket, sir," he said.

"I don't have one," Brass said. "I figured to purchase one from you."

"Where are you going?" the conductor said.

"The gentleman up front by the window,

where is he going?" Brass said.

Topeka, Kansas, 1883
In the back room of a saloon, Bat Masterson, Wyatt Earp, Charlie Bassett, and Luke Short sat at a table, sipped drinks, and played cards.

"What are we waiting on?" Bassett said.

Masterson looked at the door as it opened and Tillman walked in. "Him," Masterson said.

"Why, hello, Sam," Earp said.

"Got your telegram and took the train here," Tillman said.

"Have a seat, Sam," Masterson said. "We'll fill you in."

Tillman took a chair next to Earp, and Earp poured him a drink.

"Sam, you know Charlie Bassett?" Masterson said. "He founded the Long Branch Saloon in Dodge City."

"Sure. How are you, Charlie?" Tillman said.

"I've seen better days, Sam," Bassett said.

"Now Luke Short is part owner of the Long Branch, and Lawrence Deger, the new mayor of Dodge City, has ordered all saloons and gambling halls in Dodge to be closed," Masterson said.

"I heard something about that a year ago

or so," Tillman said.

"Well, he did it," Short said. "Locked everything up tight and tossed me in jail for no reason. Me and Charlie are legitimate business owners, and that crazy son of a bitch just shut us down."

"I talked to the governor," Masterson said. "Dodge City is an important cattle town. The Santa Fe Railroad does a lot of business in Dodge. Cowboys need a place to let off steam after a long drive. The governor would not like it if the Santa Fe moved its operation to Nebraska because Deger is on a mission to turn Dodge City into Boston."

"Has there been bloodshed?" Tillman said.

"Some," Masterson said. "Deger employs gun hands and thugs to enforce his laws. Jack Bridges and Louis Hartman to name a few."

"Those two," Tillman said.

"You know them?" Masterson said.

"Cowards, the both of them," Tillman said.

"The governor would like this issue resolved peacefully," Masterson said. "If at all possible."

"Train leaves in thirty minutes," Earp said. "We'll be in Dodge by four this afternoon."

■ ■ ■ ■

Dodge City, 1883

At the Dodge City railroad depot, Tillman retrieved his horse from the boxcar as Masterson, Earp, Bassett, and Short waited on the platform.

"Wyatt," Masterson said.

"I see them," Earp said. "Charlie, Luke, stay in the background."

Jack Bridges and three deputies walked along the platform to Earp and Masterson.

"You aren't welcome in Dodge City anymore, Masterson. You, either, Earp," Bridges said.

"On whose authority?" Earp said.

"Mayor Deger," Bridges said.

"We'll see about that," Masterson said.

"This ain't your territory anymore, Masterson," Bridges said. "You, neither, Earp. Now get back on the train and get out of here before I . . ."

"Before you what?" Tillman said as he walked his horse to Bridges.

"Who are you?" Bridges said.

"United States Marshal Sam Tillman, and my territory is wherever the hell I happen to be standing," Tillman said. "And you are obstructing justice."

"I don't know what that means," Bridges said.

"Allow me to explain it to you then," Tillman said, as he drew his Colt and smacked Bridges across the head with it.

Aiming the Colt at the three deputies, Tillman said, "Bat, Wyatt, get their guns and put them on the train."

Once Bridges and the three deputies were safely on the train, Tillman said, "Which of you is better with a rifle?"

"Wyatt is," Masterson said.

"Wyatt, you take my Winchester and watch the rooftops," Tillman said. "Bat, help yourself to my scattergun."

"They'll know we'll be coming," Masterson said.

"I know, but it won't matter," Tillman said.

Holding his horse by the reins, Tillman led Earp and Masterson to Main Street. At the end of the street an overturned wagon protected three of Deger's men.

"I see one on the roof with a rifle and another in the alley between the Long Branch and the freight office," Tillman said. "Occupy them for me while I take care of those at the wagon."

"What do you mean 'take care of'?" Masterson said.

Without answering, Tillman mounted his horse and charged toward the wagon.

"There he goes," Earp said. "Best cover him."

When he reached the wagon, Tillman jumped his horse clear over it, shocking the three men behind it.

Before they reacted, Tillman turned this horse, aimed his Colt, and shot two of them dead.

The third man tossed down his gun.

"Where's the mayor?" Tillman said.

"In his office."

"Get up and get out of here," Tillman said. "And by that, I mean clear out of Dodge City."

Lawrence Deger sat behind his desk and stared at Tillman, Earp, and Masterson.

"You will not get away with this," Deger said.

"I'm afraid you have that backwards," Masterson said.

"The governor of Kansas wants a peaceful solution to this situation, and you're going to give it to him, or so help me God, I'll drag you by the seat of your pants to the capitol, and you'll answer to him personally," Tillman said.

"The saloons will reopen and the rightful

owners will be allowed to conduct business," Masterson said. "By authority of the governor, if you fail to comply, you will be removed from office. Is that clear?"

Deger sighed and then nodded.

"One more thing," Tillman said. "I am appointing Bat Masterson and Wyatt Earp town marshals in Dodge until a new and honest sheriff can be elected. Please don't force me to return because, if I have to, I'll bring half the marshals in the service with me and you'll go to prison for obstruction. Am I clear on the matter?"

Deger nodded again. "Crystal," he said.

"Good," Tillman said. "Bat, Wyatt, let's go over to the Long Branch and have us a drink."

Tillman didn't realize he was dozing until he opened his eyes and his head was against the window.

The newspaper still lay on his lap. He adjusted his reading glasses and glanced at the page he had been reading. The headline was *Champion Jeffries in Omaha*. The byline was Bat Masterson.

Tillman grinned and took the newspaper with him to the dining car. He ordered a steak with potatoes, put on his glasses, and continued reading the newspaper while he ate.

As he lingered a bit over a cup of coffee, Tillman smoked his pipe and let his mind wander a bit.

"Is everything all right, sir?" a waiter said.

"Fine," Tillman said. "What time is breakfast served?"

"Starts at six in the morning."

"And what time do we arrive in Fort Smith?"

"The scheduled stop is ten a.m.," the waiter said.

"I shall see you for breakfast," Tillman said.

CHAPTER ELEVEN

Tillman sat in the chair in his riding car and smoked his pipe. He removed the flask from his jacket pocket and took a sip of whiskey.

The movement of the train and the whiskey had a lulling effect, so Tillman closed his eyes and allowed his thoughts to wander again.

The Big Woods of Wisconsin

For the first twenty-one years of his life, home for Sam Tillman was the "Big Woods" of Wisconsin.

His father owned a small farm in the Big Woods and grew primarily wheat and corn. They also raised pigs and chickens and kept milking cows for milk and butter. Summers were hot, winters were cold and snowy. Fall was a beautiful array of colors, and spring was muddy.

His father's name was Charles; his mother

was Margaret. They were Scotch and Irish and migrated to America in 1820, when they were in their early teens. They didn't know each other until they met on the ship carrying them to America.

Family already living in Wisconsin helped them get settled. They married, bought sixty acres of farmland, and in 1840 Sam was born. Alice came three years later.

By the time he was six, Tillman was helping his father with chores after school. He milked the cows, churned butter with his mother, and pitched hay in the barn.

Every morning when school was in session, Tillman walked Alice to the one-room schoolhouse in town. She started school when she was six. By then Tillman was a growing body of nine, and he had the shoulders of a man.

Mary Elizabeth came into his life when her family moved to the Big Woods from Minnesota and purchased the farm that abutted theirs.

Mary Elizabeth was a year younger than Sam, and Tillman and Alice would wait for her on the road and walk together to school. His father told him it was his job to keep them safe. From what, Tillman had no idea, but he took his task seriously.

In the spring of his tenth year, Tillman

found out from what when he walked his sister and Mary Elizabeth home from school. A man attacked them.

The man was a stranger in the Big Woods. He was seen a few times camping by the creek, but he never stayed in one spot for very long, and most folks paid him no mind.

He made his intentions known when he appeared from behind a large tree and attempted to kidnap Mary Elizabeth. The man was twice Tillman's size at the time, knocked him to the ground, grabbed Mary Elizabeth, and carried her off to the woods.

Tillman sent Alice ahead to fetch their father and then pursued the man down to the creek.

Tillman had the jackknife his father had given him for his tenth birthday. He raced up to the kidnapper and stabbed him several times in the back.

The man released Mary Elizabeth and turned to Tillman. The kidnapper grabbed Tillman. Tillman stabbed him several more times in the chest before the man knocked him to the ground.

The kidnapper sat on Tillman's stomach and grabbed the jackknife from Tillman's hand. He was about to shove the blade into Tillman's chest, when Tillman's father arrived and shot the man dead with his plains rifle.

It was later learned that the man was wanted in several states for kidnapping, murder, and assaulting a child.

Battered and bruised, Tillman walked Mary Elizabeth home that afternoon. At her house, she announced that when they came of age, she was going to marry Tillman.

Residents in the Big Woods celebrated Tillman as a hero for his courage in saving Mary Elizabeth, but Tillman never spoke of the incident except to the local sheriff, who needed to make a report.

For his twelfth birthday, Tillman's father bought him a plains rifle, a .50 caliber cap-and-ball Hawken, exactly like the one his father had.

His father taught Tillman to shoot. In the spring of his twelfth year, Tillman hunted and killed his first deer.

In the summer months, Tillman worked the farm full-time with his father. By the time he was fourteen, Tillman was taller and broader than his father. This didn't go unnoticed by the young women in the Big Woods at the local dances.

But Tillman was not interested in any girl other than Mary Elizabeth, who was a budding young woman in her own right.

By the time he reached sixteen, Tillman could ride a horse as well as any man, and he taught himself to shoot his father's 1851 Navy Colt pistol from the saddle, a skill that would serve him many times in his life. He finished his schooling that same year, and his family talked about sending him to attend the university in Milwaukee when he turned eighteen.

The family saved money for his tuition by saving every penny they could. Tillman took every odd job in town he could find to support the cause.

On his eighteenth birthday, the family and Mary Elizabeth made the trip to Milwaukee to enroll Tillman in the university.

He was an excellent student in the first year. The second year was dominated by talk of war, and the inevitable fracturing of the country that was soon to follow.

A free state from its inception, Wisconsin was a major force for abolitionism. When war erupted, more than ninety thousand men, Tillman included, enlisted into the Union Army.

The day before he was scheduled to report to New York for training, Tillman married Mary Elizabeth in a small, private ceremony at the local church.

Mary Elizabeth and both families saw him

off at the railroad station in Milwaukee. The new bride, his sister, and mother cried like babies.

His father told him to do his duty to his country.

1901

Tillman took a final sip from the flask, set it aside, and entered the bed in the riding car. Sometimes, at night, when he was alone and things were quiet, he could almost smell the soap on Mary Elizabeth's skin and hair. Feel the warmth of her skin next to his under the covers, hear her shallow breathing as she slept.

A finer woman God never created.

Or took.

He looked up at the dark ceiling.

She'd been gone twenty years, but was still always with him.

"To the very good days of long ago," he said.

CHAPTER TWELVE

Tillman found an empty table in the dining car and ordered coffee before breakfast. He was drinking coffee and skimming a newspaper when a woman of about twenty came up to the table.

"Excuse me, sir," she said.

"Yes, miss?" Tillman said.

"Every table is occupied, and this is the only vacant seat," the woman said. "May I sit with you for breakfast?"

"Yes, of course," Tillman said.

He stood to move the chair back to allow the young woman to sit.

"Thank you, sir," she said. "My name is Lauren Blair."

"Sam Tillman," Tillman said as he took his chair.

"I see by your badge that you are a US Marshal," Lauren said.

"For three more weeks, anyway," Tillman said.

"Are you retiring, sir?" Lauren said.

"A man my age has no business being a marshal," Tillman said. "I figure thirty years is enough."

Lauren smiled. "I bet you have some wonderful stories to tell," she said.

"Everybody has a story in them to tell," Tillman said. "Even one so young as you."

"I'm afraid my story is rather boring," Lauren said.

"A pretty, educated young woman like you? The whole world is in front of you," Tillman said. "Your story is only on page one."

"My world is being the daughter of a wealthy cattle baron in Omaha," Lauren said. "I've attended boarding school since the age of eight. After boarding school came finishing school. I wanted to attend a university, but my parents don't believe a woman should attend a university because my place is to marry and produce heirs."

"I'm sure they want only what's best for you," Tillman said.

"I'm sure they do, except that I don't want what they want," Lauren said. "I don't wish to marry the son of another cattle baron, or a banker or a lawyer. I want to travel and see the world first before I marry, and when I do marry, it will be for love and not money."

"Those are fine words to live by," Tillman said.

"Listen to me drone on," Lauren said.

"Not at all," Tillman said. "I enjoy talking to young people."

"You must be married with a family," Lauren said. "Does your wife mind you being away from home all the time?"

"My wife got used to me being away from home during the war," Tillman said. "I was gone for three and a half years in the war, you see."

"I haven't met very many who actually fought in the war," Lauren said. "Most of the men my parents try to marry me off to are nothing but boys."

"It's different times, these days," Tillman said.

The waiter came to the table. "Are you ready to order?" he said.

"I'll have steak and eggs," Tillman said. "Medium on the steak, scrambled on the eggs. Orange juice and coffee."

Lauren looked at the waiter. "Make that two," she said.

"Is that your usual breakfast?" Tillman said.

"Toast with two poached eggs is my usual breakfast," Lauren said. "As boring as my life is, I'm afraid."

"May I give you some advice?" Tillman said.

"Please."

"Do what your heart tells you to do, and to hell with what others think," Tillman said. "Others can't live your life for you, and that includes your parents."

Lauren sipped coffee as she thought for a moment. "That is very frightening to me," she said. "You see, I'm spoiled by my family's wealth. If I follow my heart, I will be poor, and that scares me terribly."

"It's not an easy thing to do to follow your heart," Tillman said. "If a certain group of people didn't follow theirs, we'd all be drinking tea and paying taxes to a king of England."

"You make me ashamed of myself, Marshal Tillman," Lauren said. "Because I'm weak and choose the money."

"You are also very young and have time to figure it all out," Tillman said.

The waiter arrived with breakfast.

"I've never had steak and eggs for breakfast," Lauren said.

"Well, young lady, that's a start," Tillman said.

"Are you going to Fort Smith?" Lauren said as she sliced into her steak.

"Yes, visiting an old friend." Tillman. said. "Are you?"

"Just long enough to connect to the train to Florida," Lauren said. "My family has a house in the town of Miami. I'm meeting my older brother there for several weeks. We only use the house in winter, but mother wants it painted."

With breakfast finished, Tillman, out of courtesy, paid Lauren's bill.

"That wasn't necessary, Marshal," she said. "I have ample funds with me."

"That isn't the point," Tillman said. "And that's something else you'll need to figure out."

The train began to slow its speed.

"We should be in the station in about fifteen minutes," Tillman said. "I best return to my cabin and get my things."

"I'll need to do the same," Lauren said.

As Tillman walked Blue along the platform, he found Lauren waiting for him.

"I believe I've never seen so large a horse for riding," she said.

"A smarter animal you'll never meet," Tillman said.

"My connecting train doesn't arrive for thirty minutes," Lauren said. "I wonder if you might sit with me for a bit."

"A lady should never wait unattended," Tillman said.

He tethered Blue to the hitching post at the end of the platform, and then he and Lauren took seats on a bench.

"Have you been to Fort Smith before?" Tillman said.

"Only to connect trains," Lauren said.

"New York and Boston?"

"Many times," Lauren said. "And Chicago, Saint Louis, and even Paris once with my mother."

"And Fort Smith scares you," Tillman said.

Lauren looked at Tillman. "I'm that obvious?"

"A young, pretty woman traveling alone should always be on her guard for the expected and the unexpected," Tillman said.

"Is that professional or personal advice?" Lauren said.

"Call it both," Tillman said.

"I see my train coming," Lauren said.

"Well, young lady, I wish you the best, and I hope you find in life what you are looking for," Tillman said.

Tillman waited with Lauren for the train to arrive and, after a porter took her bags on board, Lauren smiled and said, "I do envy your wife, Marshal Tillman. Tell her that for me."

CHAPTER THIRTEEN

Fort Smith, Arkansas, 1875

By July of 1875, Tillman was a full-fledged United States Marshal with federal authority in all states and territories.

Glen Post, recovering from a leg injury, was assigned to a desk job as an assistant to a regional supervisor in Washington. When a request from a federal judge came across his desk, Post took it to his superior for a recommendation.

They both agreed that Tillman was the man for the job and sent him from his home in Colorado to Fort Smith in Arkansas to report to Judge Isaac Parker.

The temporary position came with a boost in pay to six hundred and fifty dollars a month. For the past several years, Tillman had been buying up land in Montana at twenty dollars an acre for the purpose of building a ranch. He and Mary Elizabeth wanted a real home where they could raise their two boys and, hopefully, a couple of girls.

They started buying land in Montana when Tillman worked for the railroad as chief of police at a very inflated salary.

Before leaving Colorado, they discussed the move to Fort Smith. The extra money would buy additional acres quicker, but Mary Elizabeth didn't fancy living in such a lawless town.

As they stood on the platform after leaving the train, Mary Elizabeth took one look around and said, "Sam, what a shithole of a town."

"I've seen worse," Tillman said.

"Where? Hell?" Mary Elizabeth said.

Even as a child, Mary Elizabeth didn't mince words. She spoke her mind and could swear with the best of them when provoked.

"It's just a temporary assignment," Tillman said. "And that extra money will buy a lot of acres."

"Get your horse, and let's see where we will be living," Mary Elizabeth said.

Tillman retrieved his horse from the boxcar. Together they walked through wide, muddy streets filled with cowboys and freight wagons.

Situated on the Arkansas River, Fort Smith was established as a trade route and later an army outpost. Although the outpost closed after the Civil War, Fort Smith was still an important trade route. It was even more so now, with the railroad established.

Most of the structures were wood, but one building made of stone dominated the entire town: the courthouse.

"The letter from Washington said our house is a block behind the courthouse," Tillman said. "Do you have the letter?"

"In my handbag," Mary Elizabeth said. She dug the letter out and scanned through it. "Ten Courthouse Way," she said.

"Let's head toward the courthouse," Tillman said.

"Are the streets always muddy like this?" Mary Elizabeth said.

"I expect they are after a hard rain," Tillman said.

They reached the courthouse. It was odd seeing so dominant a building in such a small town.

"I don't see a church or a school," Mary Elizabeth said.

"I'm sure they have them," Tillman said.

They followed Courthouse Way to the edge of town, where a gray and yellow house with a white picket fence was being worked on by several men.

"Is this number Ten Courthouse Way?"

Tillman said to a man on the roof.

"It is, sir," the man said and jumped down. "We're getting it ready for a new marshal."

"That would be me," Tillman said.

The man looked at Tillman's badge. "Go on in and check the place out," the man said. "We spent two days cleaning it for you."

Tillman and Mary Elizabeth entered the house. It was neat and clean and fully furnished, with two bedrooms, a large kitchen and parlor, and a separate room for dining.

"We'll need an extra bed for Glen," Mary Elizabeth said. "Jake is too big now to sleep with his brother."

"We'll check in town," Tillman said. "My parents aren't bringing the boys for another week."

"What about school and church?"

"I'll ask the judge. I'm sure he knows," Tillman said.

The man Tillman had spoken to entered the house. "We have a few repairs left on the roof," he said. "Otherwise, she's complete."

"Our luggage is being delivered by the railroad," Tillman said. "Can you see it gets brought inside?"

"Sure thing, Marshal," the man said.

"And where are you going?" Mary Elizabeth said.

"The courthouse to meet my new boss," Tillman said.

Judge Isaac Parker, newly appointed by President Grant, wasn't more than a few years older than Tillman, but appeared far older due to his white hair and beard. He stood eight inches shorter than Tillman, but had a way about him that made a person respect the man's authority.

"Sam. May I call you Sam?" Parker said.

"It's my name, Judge," Tillman said.

"Have a seat," Parker said.

Tillman sat in a chair opposite the desk.

Parker stood and walked to a cabinet against the wall. He opened the cabinet, filled two shot glasses with bourbon, and returned to the desk. He gave one glass to Tillman and then took his chair.

"Sam, I've been entrusted with a district that covers a third of the state and the entire Indian Nation on both sides of the border," Parker said. "This town, this territory, has the makings of a fine, decent place for families to live and grow. At the present time, this territory, including the Indian Nation, is overrun with outlaws. Murderers, thieves, and rapists of the worst sort. My job, my responsibility, is to clean this place up and make it a respectable community for folks to raise their families in."

Tillman took a sip of his drink.

"I asked Washington for the best marshal they have, and they sent me you," Parker said. "And although you are federal and not district, they agreed to let me borrow you, so to speak, to help me with my task."

"That's how it was explained to me," Tillman said.

"So you have no problem working for a judge?" Parker said.

"If I did, I would have refused the job," Tillman said.

"Good. Good. Sam, I have a staff of very inexperienced marshals," Parker said. "I need you to show them the way."

"I'll do what I can," Tillman said.

"One marshal shows particular promise," Parker said. "His name is Bass Reeves. I'd like you to work with him closely. He's green, but an excellent tracker."

"Like I said, I'll do what I can," Tillman said.

"Sam, he's a Negro. Is that a problem for you?" Parker said.

"I'm not a Negro. Is that a problem for him?" Tillman said.

Parker smiled. "Your record states you enlisted at the start of the war out of Wisconsin. I expect it's not a problem for either."

"When can I meet the man, and what's our first assignment?" Tillman said.

"I'll expect you'll meet him by the time you get home," Parker said. "He lives a few houses down from yours. I'll have your first assignment in the morning."

"Good enough, Judge," Tillman said.

"I hope the house is adequate for your wife and boys," Parker said.

"It will do nicely," Tillman said. "Oh, by the way, my wife wants to know about schools and a church."

"We have a nice one of both," Parker said.

When Tillman returned to Ten Courthouse Way, five black children were playing in the front yard.

"Howdy, kids," Tillman said.

"Are you the new marshal?" a boy of about ten said.

"I am," Tillman said.

"Ma and Pa are inside waiting on you," the boy said.

"Thank you kindly," Tillman said.

When Tillman entered the house, Mary Elizabeth, Bass Reeves, and his wife, Nellie, were having coffee in the parlor.

Reeves stood as Tillman approached the table.

"Sam, this is Marshal Bass Reeves and his wife, Nellie," Mary Elizabeth said.

Tillman and Reeves shook hands.

"All those kids yours?" Tillman said.

"With one more on the way," Reeves said.

"Marshal Tillman, do me a favor and take Bass on assignment," Nellie said. "So my body can get some rest."

"Sam, why don't you and Marshal Reeves take coffee on the porch?" Mary Elizabeth said.

Tillman and Reeves sat in chairs on the porch and watched Reeves's five children play in the yard.

Tillman lit his pipe.

"I count five," he said.

"One more on the way," Reeves said. "Your wife said you got two boys."

"She'd like a girl or two," Tillman said.

"They all do, so they can dress them up like dolls," Reeves said.

"I expect you're right."

"Do you know why Judge Parker picked me for a marshal?" Reeves said.

"He said you show particular promise," Tillman said.

"I was born a slave to Mr. William Reeves in Crawford County, Arkansas," Reeves said. "When he moved to Texas, I escaped during the war and lived in the Indian Nation until the war ended. I speak five Indian languages and learned to track from the Cherokee, Seminole, and Creek tribes. The judge wants men who can track. I can track."

"What did you do after the war until now?" Tillman said.

"Farmed rented land," Reeves said. "To tell you the truth, I was no damn good at it. No good at it at all."

"I can say the same for myself," Tillman said.

"You? Where?"

"Place called the Big Woods in Wisconsin," Tillman said. "My folks grew wheat and corn. I grew mud, calluses, and sweat."

"Wisconsin was an abolitionist state," Reeves said.

"It was," Tillman said. "And many a slave came through Wisconsin on the way to Canada. My folks took several in and helped them make it north at great risk to them, neighbors, and their kids. Gave them food and water for the journey."

"You fought for the Union?"

"Me and ninety thousand others out of

Wisconsin."

"See much action?"

"My fair share, I expect."

Tillman puffed on his pipe and then sipped some coffee. "Let me ask you something, Bass. Have you ever killed a man?"

"No. I beat up Mr. Reeves to escape, but I've never killed," Reeves said.

"Well, better set your mind to the fact that killing comes with that badge you're wearing," Tillman said.

"I expect it does," Reeves said.

"But that's a subject for another day," Tillman said.

The door opened and Mary Elizabeth and Nellie came outside.

"Bass, gather the kids," Nellie said. "I'm sure Mary Elizabeth and the marshal have a lot to do."

"Let's have breakfast in the morning," Tillman said. "We'll walk over and see the judge afterward."

As she put her clothes into the dresser, Mary Elizabeth said, "Bass is a nice person, Sam. So is Nellie. He's not a lawman, not yet. It's up to you to teach him and make sure he doesn't get killed."

Seated on the bed, Tillman stared at Mary Elizabeth.

"Did you hear me, Sam?" Mary Elizabeth said.

"I did, but right now I'm thinking more about maybe making us a daughter," Tillman said.

Mary Elizabeth paused and turned around. "You best not give me another boy," she said. "Two is about all I can handle."

CHAPTER FOURTEEN

Fort Smith, Arkansas, 1901

Fort Smith had grown into an enormous town of twelve thousand residents. The wide streets were clean, and many of the buildings were made of brick instead of wood. Telegraph poles lined several of the larger streets in the center of town.

Electric lights provided light for many of the businesses and homes.

Wagons and carriages clogged the streets, and Tillman drew stares as he rode Blue onto Main Street toward the courthouse.

At the courthouse, Tillman stopped at the corral. At one time, dozens of horses belonging to district marshals filled the corral.

Today there were just three.

Tillman opened the gate and put Blue in with the three. The three horses, intimidated by Blue's size, backed away from him.

"Try not to step on these here girls," Tillman told Blue.

As he walked toward the rear entrance of the courthouse, the heavy metal door leading to the holding jail opened, and a district marshal stepped out.

"The corral is reserved for marshals and court officers," he said.

"Of which I am one of," Tillman said. He moved his jacket to display his badge. "Marshal Sam Tillman."

The district marshal stared at Tillman. "The Sam Tillman I heard so much about?"

"Unless I have a long-lost twin," Tillman said. "I'm looking for Bass Reeves and Cal Whitson. Are they about?"

"In the courthouse, on the second floor."

"Obliged."

Tillman walked up the steps to the rear door of the courthouse. The door wasn't locked, so he opened it and stepped inside.

In the lobby, a young deputy sat behind a desk and guarded a metal gate. A typewriter, a phone, and a logbook were on the desk.

"May I help you?" the young deputy said.

"Marshal Sam Tillman to see Bass Reeves and Cal Whitson," Tillman said.

"You'll have to check your sidearm," the young deputy said.

"Check it for what?" Tillman said.

"Leave it here with me. Firearms aren't permitted inside the courthouse."

"Is that a phone you have there?"

"It is."

"Use it to call Bass or Whitson and tell them I'm in the lobby."

The young deputy stared at Tillman.

"Son, my horse is older than you," Tillman said.

The young deputy picked up the receiver and cranked the handle on the phone. "Let me speak to Marshal Reeves or Whitson," he said.

A few moments passed and the young deputy said, "Marshal Sam Tillman." The young deputy looked at Tillman and then said, "He doesn't want to check his firearm."

The young deputy looked at Tillman. "He hung up," he said.

"Well, what does that mean?" Tillman said.

"I don't . . ." the young deputy said.

A door behind the metal gate opened and Reeves and Whitson stepped out.

"Open that gate, pup," Whitson said.

"It's against courthouse rules to allow —"

"Oh, shut up and open the gate," Whitson said.

The young deputy hit a lever and then slid the gate open. Reeves and Whitson walked past the desk to Tillman.

"Son of a bitch, Bass, it really is Sam Tillman," Whitson said.

Tillman shook hands with Reeves and Whitson.

"What brings you to Fort Smith, Sam?" Reeves said.

"Can we get out of this dungeon? Maybe grab a cup of coffee?" Tillman said.

"Sonny, we'll be back," Whitson said.

"What if the judge looks for you?" the young deputy said.

"Tell him we went fishing," Reeves said.

"Why aren't you retired yet, Sam?" Whitson said.

They were in a small café not far from the courthouse. People at other tables stared at Tillman as they drank their coffee.

"In three weeks I will be," Tillman said. "After that, I'm a full-time rancher."

"What brings you to town?" Reeves said.

"Passing through on one final assignment," Tillman said. "Thought I'd stop off and see you boys on the way."

"It sure is good to see you, Sam," Reeves said. "How are your boys?"

"Fine men working the ranch," Tillman said. "And yours?"

"All eleven are just fine," Reeves said. "My boy Homer is a junior deputy."

Tillman lit his pipe and looked across the table at Reeves and Whitson. Reeves, a few years older than Tillman, wasn't as stout as he once was, but still appeared in good health and his eyes were as sharp as ever.

Whitson, a tall, slender man in his mid-fifties, wore an eye patch over his left eye where he was wounded in battle during the Civil War.

"How are things since old Parker passed?" Tillman said.

"Quiet since the judge has been gone," Whitson said. "Civilization has come to Fort Smith at last."

"I noticed," Tillman said.

"Folks don't go heeled anymore, and crime is a thing of the past," Reeves said. "I was thinking of retiring come next winter."

"Gentlemen, that's called progress," Tillman said.

"I call it old age," Reeves said.

Across the street from the small café, Brass sat on a bench in the Courthouse Square and sketched in his notebook.

As he watched the three men through the window, Brass titled the sketch he was drawing "Marshals Having Coffee in Fort Smith."

Brass knew the black marshal as Bass

Reeves, the famous once-a-slave marshal in Judge Parker's court of the old days.

He wasn't sure who the marshal with the eye patch was, but he could always look that up later.

While Brass was making notes, Tillman, Reeves, and the marshal with the eye patch came out of the café.

Tillman shook hands with the marshal wearing the eye patch and then Tillman and Reeves went one way, and the marshal with the eye patch went another.

Brass waited until the marshal with the eye patch walked past the park, and then he stood and followed Tillman and Reeves.

The block where Ten Courthouse Way once stood was now lined with a large freight warehouse that extended the entire block.

"When did they tear all the old houses down?" Tillman said.

"In ninety-seven, after the judge died," Reeves said. "I miss the old son of a bitch."

"The Hanging Judge was a good man all right," Tillman said. "I'm sure he has a first-class ticket upstairs."

"I'm not so sure I like these modern times," Reeves said.

"I know what you mean, Bass," Tillman said. "Like a way of life is gone and is never coming back."

"The house we live in now has an indoor toilet," Reeves said. "My wife got one of those iceboxes in the kitchen with a block of ice in the bottom. I'd like to know what's next."

"Electric lights and horseless carriages," Tillman said.

"My ass," Reeves said.

Tillman grinned. "Bass, my old friend, we've been lawmen too long," he said.

"Ain't that the truth," Reeves said.

"I need to get my horse and find a hotel for the night," Tillman said.

"The Piccadilly is the best in town," Reeves said. "Opened in ninety-eight."

"Do they have a livery?" Tillman said.

"No, but the livery on West Street is still in business," Reeves said. "Let's get your horse and your room, and you can have dinner at my house."

"That's the best offer I've had in a month," Tillman said.

CHAPTER FIFTEEN

Fort Smith, Arkansas, 1875

Tillman and Reeves sat in chairs in Judge Parker's office and waited while he filled out warrants.

There was a coffee pot on the woodstove, and Tillman filled two cups and gave one to Reeves.

Finally, Parker looked up. "I have six warrants here," he said. "Two for the Kincaid brothers, Joe and Jack. Four unknown. They robbed the bank in Little Rock and killed the guard, a manager, and a deputy. They also robbed the bank in Pine Bluff, and are suspected of robbing two banks in Texas and several stagecoaches. It is believed they stopped in Fort Smith for supplies and are now hiding out in the Indian Nation."

"We best get after them then," Tillman said.

"How many deputies do you figure you'll need?" Parker said.

"Just the two of us should do," Tillman said.

Reeves turned his head and looked at Tillman.

"The two of you can't go after six dangerous men alone," Parker said. "These men are killers, and I doubt they'd hesitate to kill again."

"Judge, if we go traipsing around the Ozark Mountains with a large posse, we might as well bring a bugle and set off flares. We have to track these men, and do it quietly," Tillman said.

"What do you say, Bass?" Parker said.

"I think I agree with Sam," Reeves said.

Parker sighed. "All right, but I'm against it. Get supplies, and whatever else you need at the general store and have them bill the court."

Tillman grabbed the warrants. "Don't worry, Judge, we'll try to bring them in alive," he said.

"Try to bring yourselves in alive," Parker said.

As they walked over to the general store, Tillman said, "Bass, what do you got in your holster there?"

"A Remington .38," Reeves said.

"Got a rifle?" Tillman said.

"Don't own one," Reeves said.

"Nothing like a well-equipped army," Tillman said.

At the general store, Reeves drew stares from customers, but no one said anything and the clerk didn't object to waiting on them. After ordering supplies to last three weeks, Tillman said, "The marshal here needs a Colt revolver, the best you have in the store."

"I have some new Peacemakers, but they won't fit that Remington holster," the clerk said.

"Then we'll take the holster along with it," Tillman said. "And a Winchester '73 for Marshal Reeves."

Wearing his new Colt and carrying the new Winchester '73, Reeves grinned at Tillman as they walked home.

"Think the judge will be mad?" Reeves said.

"A district marshal can't be expected to bring outlaws to justice with just a Remington .38," Tillman said. "The judge said to bring ourselves in alive. The best way to do that is with the proper equipment."

When they reached Courthouse Way, Tillman said, "We'll leave first thing in the morning."

■ ■ ■ ■

As they rode west of Fort Smith, Reeves said, "Do you always ride so large a horse?"

"A habit I picked up during the war," Tillman said.

"When we reach the foothills, I'd like to try my new Colt and Winchester," Reeves said.

"When do we reach the foothills?" Tillman said.

"Late this afternoon, after we cross the Arkansas River," Reeves said.

"We'll try them both after breakfast in the morning," Tillman said. "We cross on a river raft?"

"One dollar for a person, a dollar-fifty per horse," Reeves said.

"That's highway robbery," Tillman said.

"Ain't no other way to cross the Arkansas when the water is up," Reeves said.

They reached the river raft by four in the afternoon. Four men waited on the raft for customers. An old woman sat on the porch of a small cabin.

"We're looking to cross," Tillman said.

"Pay Ma," one of the four men said.

"Be right back," Tillman said and rode his horse to the cabin. "Two for crossing," he said to Ma.

Ma was easily seventy years old and was chewing tobacco and spitting the juice into a tin can. "Six dollars," she said.

"Your sign there says two-fifty for man and horse," Tillman said.

"We don't usually take darkies, but I see you both wear a badge," Ma said. "Six dollars. Take it or leave it."

"Poor treatment of a lawman, if you ask me," Tillman said.

"I didn't," Ma said. "And it's still six dollars."

"We're looking for six men who might have crossed the river the past week or so," Tillman said.

"Kincaid brothers?" Ma said.

"Those are the ones."

"About a week, maybe six days ago," Ma said.

Tillman paid Ma with a ten-dollar bill and told her to keep the change — payment for the information. Then he rode back to the raft. "Let's go," he said to Reeves.

It took the four men nearly thirty minutes to pull the raft across the three-quarters-of-a-mile-wide river. Two men on each side of the raft pulled thick ropes. The work was hard and slow.

After exiting the raft, Tillman said, "Ma

said the Kincaid brothers crossed the river a week ago."

"Probably going for the gorge in the Indian Nation where they can hide out for as long as they want," Reeves said.

"We got two hours of daylight left, then we'll find us a place to make camp," Tillman said.

Reeves took them to a shallow creek in the foothills where they made camp. They built a fire and put on a pan of beans along with fresh slices of meat and then tended to the horses.

"Any ideas on a direction we should follow?" Tillman said as he stirred the pan.

"We'll head up to the Cherokee Nation, and I'll have a talk with a couple of friends," Reeves said. "They might have seen them in their travels."

Tillman removed a bottle of whiskey from his gear and added an ounce to the pan. "For flavor," he said.

"Mister Reeves used to have Fourth of July cookouts at his place, and he would put whiskey on all the meats and sauces," Reeves said.

"Did they teach you to read?" Tillman said.

"No, my wife did after we got married," Reeves said. "She was a house slave and needed to read, so they taught her."

"You didn't meet until after the war?" Tillman said.

"After I left the Cherokee and took up farming," Reeves said. "What about your missus?"

"I was lucky so fine a woman took a shine to me when we were just kids back in Wisconsin," Tillman said. "Let's eat, Marshal Bass. I'm hungry."

In the morning, while a half pound of bacon sizzled in a pan and biscuits warmed beside a fire, Reeves tried out his new Colt Peacemaker.

"The Peacemaker is the perfect instrument of law enforcement," Tillman said. "And you have to treat it as gentle as you would your wife. First hold it and get the feel of its balance."

Reeves removed the Colt from the holster and got the feel of it in his right hand.

"That tree about seventy-five yards in front of you is about as wide as a man," Tillman said. "Put six into the bark."

Reeves cocked the Colt and took aim.

"No, don't aim. Shoot. Aiming is for the Winchester at long distances," Tillman said.

Reeves looked at the tree. "Just shoot?" he said.

"Point and shoot," Tillman said. "And be quick about it, or the man shooting back will gain the advantage."

Reeves pointed the Colt and fired six shots at the trunk of the tree. Four bullets found the mark, although they were scattered.

"I missed two," Reeves said.

"The four you hit would have killed or disabled the man on the other end of it," Tillman said. "That's your concern."

"How good are you?" Reeves said.

Tillman drew his Colt and rapid-fired six shots into the tree in a grouping six inches wide.

"I guess I have some work to do," Reeves said.

"How are you with a long gun?" Tillman said.

"I can hit a bird flying," Reeves said.

"Good, because you just might have to," Tillman said. "Feel like some eggs?"

Tillman removed a tin box from the gear and opened it to reveal two dozen eggs.

"We're close," Reeves said.

"Good, because I'm sick of riding these damned hills," Tillman said.

Reeves stopped his horse, and Tillman stopped beside him.

Speaking in Cherokee, Reeves said, "I am

Bass Reeves of the Cherokee Nation. Show yourself."

Tillman looked around and saw nothing.

Then, from behind a tree, a Cherokee warrior stepped out. "Who is the big ugly white man?" Joseph Walking Stick said in Cherokee.

"My partner," Reeves said in Cherokee. "We need your help. Can we come to camp?"

"Come. Two Crows will be pleased to see you again," Joseph Walking Stick said in Cherokee.

Tillman and Reeves followed Joseph Walking Stick down a hill to where his horse was tethered to a tree.

"Don't speak unless Two Crows speaks to you directly," Reeves said. "Otherwise, he'll be insulted. He may be a Christian, but he's still Cherokee."

While some on the outskirts chose to live in tipis, most of the Cherokee tribe lived in cabins made of wood, many with stone fireplaces and porches.

Two Crows lived in the largest cabin centered in the reservation settlement. Other notable cabins nearby were a school and a church.

Joseph Walking Stick led Reeves and

Tillman to the cabin of Two Crows, where Two Crows sat in a rocking chair on the porch. He was in his sixties, a handsome, weathered-looking man. He wore blue dungarees, a red shirt, and boots. He smoked a pipe and sipped coffee from a tin mug. A silver crucifix hung from a chain around his neck.

"Reeves, good to see you again," Two Crows said. "Who is your friend?"

"Marshal Sam Tillman," Reeves said.

"A lawman?" Two Crows said.

"A great lawman," Reeves said.

"Come have coffee with me and tell me what you want," Two Crows said.

Reeves and Tillman dismounted and went up to the porch. Joseph Walking Stick also dismounted, but he walked his horse away.

"Coffee is on the stove, Reeves," Two Crows said.

Tillman took a chair next to Two Crows while Reeves went into the cabin. Reeves returned with two mugs of coffee and gave one to Tillman.

"So, Reeves, what is the purpose of your visit?" Two Crows said.

Tillman took out his pipe and filled it with tobacco.

"Some very bad men are hiding in the nation," Reeves said. "We are hunting them."

"And you?" Two Crows said, looking at Tillman.

Tillman struck a match and lit his pipe. "These men are murderers," he said. "The worst sort of white man."

"We think they might be on the Oklahoma side, but we're not sure," Reeves said. "We'd like to know if any of your people might have seen them."

"Let's go to the church," Two Crows said.

Two Crows stood on the porch of the church, grabbed the rope, and rang the large bell overhead a dozen times.

Tillman and Reeves stood beside him.

Within a minute, a hundred Cherokee men, women, and children, including Joseph Walking Stick, stood in front of the church.

"Our old friend Bass Reeves and a marshal are tracking outlaws who are hiding in our nation," Two Crows said. "Has anybody on a hunting party seen or tracked these outlaws?"

"Six riders?" Joseph Walking Stick said.

"Yes, that's right, six riders," Reeves said.

"On the deer hunt three days ago, we spotted the tracks of six riders going west into the high country," Joseph Walking Stick said. "They were moving quickly."

"How far from here?" Reeves said.

"A day's ride," Joseph Walking Stick said.

"Tomorrow morning after the minister says Sunday service, Joseph, you will take Reeves and the marshal to the place you saw their tracks," Two Crows said.

Tillman and Reeves knew not to object and kept their mouths shut.

"Reeves, you and the marshal will eat with me tonight," Two Crows said. "The women will prepare the table in the square."

Reeves and Tillman stored their gear in a small cabin behind Two Crows's cabin.

Tillman sat in a chair at a small table in the cabin.

"We're losing a day," he said.

"That's one way of looking at it," Reeves said. "The other way is, we're saving time tracking by having Joseph take us directly to their trail."

Tillman sighed. "I guess," he said.

"Besides, it wouldn't be wise to refuse Two Crows," Reeves said. "Like I said, he may be a Christian, but he's still Cherokee."

"Well, maybe I'll take a shave and a bath before supper," Tillman said.

The table in the square held one hundred people. Reeves and Tillman sat at the end to Two Crows's left and right.

The women prepared venison stew and served it in wood bowls. Bread and biscuits made from corn were piled high on plates.

"I have eleven children and twenty-three grandchildren," Two Crows said. "Marshal Tillman, have you a family?"

"A wife and two young sons in Fort Smith," Tillman said.

"It is good we have heirs to carry on our blood," Two Crows said. "Reeves, you have how many now?"

"Five. Number six is on the way," Reeves said.

"The minister once read from the book about being fruitful and multiplying," Two Crows said. "You must have read it."

Tillman grinned. "I reckon he has taken it to heart," he said.

"I think I'll turn in," Reeves said.

"Go ahead," Tillman said. "I'm going to smoke my pipe for a while."

Tillman went outside to the porch and took a seat. He struck a match, lit his pipe, and was surprised to see Two Crows walking up the steps.

"Have you fresh tobacco?" Two Crows said as he took a chair. "Mine is a bit stale."

Tillman handed him his pouch, and Two

Crows filled his pipe. Two Crows removed a match from his shirt pocket and lit his pipe.

"Good smoke," Two Crows said. "Where is Reeves?"

"Turned in early," Tillman said.

"He's come far from his slave days," Two Crows said.

"He has that," Tillman agreed.

"You fought in the great Civil War?"

"I did."

"For the North?"

"Served under Grant, Sherman, and a few others."

"Do much killing?"

"A fair amount."

"You fought and killed your own people," Two Crows said.

"To free an enslaved race and save a country," Tillman said.

"Before your war, when my people fought your people, what defeated us most was we were fighting each other as well," Two Crows said. "You can't defeat an enemy if you are fighting each other at the same time."

"Long ago, across the Atlantic Ocean, in a city called Rome, their king, Julius Caesar, used the divide-and-conquer method to defeat many a country," Tillman said. "He called it *Divada et Impera*. Eventually, this same rule came back to bite Rome in the ass, and the Roman Empire fell apart."

"*Divida et . . .*" Two Crows said.

"*Impera,*" Tillman said.

"*Divida et Impera,*" Two Crows said.

"That is a language spoken long ago, called Latin," Tillman said.

"I will remember those words," Two Crows said. He stood up. "I will see you at breakfast before the service."

Right before breakfast was served at the table in the square, the minister arrived in a wagon full of supplies.

The supplies consisted of luxury items such as tobacco, sugar, canned fruits, medicine, school supplies, clothing and blankets, and candy for the children.

He was greeted warmly by men, women, and children alike. A special place was set for the minister beside Two Crows.

"I see you have guests," the minister said.

"Marshal Tillman and Marshal Reeves," Two Crows said. "Reeves was adopted into our nation when he was a slave and ran away during the great war."

"Will you both be staying for service?" the minister said.

"Appears so," Tillman said.

The church had room for two hundred,

and every seat was taken. Two Crows held the first seat in the right aisle. Reeves and Tillman, as guests, sat beside Two Crows. The minister spoke for forty-five minutes and concluded his service with several Psalms.

Afterward, Tillman and Reeves prepared their gear and horses and met Joseph Walking Stick in the square. Two Crows was with him.

"You can take six of my warriors with you," Two Crows said.

"Joseph will be enough," Tillman said.

"For six outlaws?" Two Crows said.

"These men are white. It wouldn't sit well with me if any of your warriors were hurt or killed if they accompany us," Tillman said.

Two Crows nodded. "Travel well. Be safe."

"I almost forgot," Tillman said. He opened a saddlebag and removed a small wood box and handed it to Two Crows. "For your hospitality and good company."

Two Crows nodded. He waited until Tillman, Reeves, and Joseph Walking Stick rode out of sight before walking to his cabin and sitting in his rocking chair and opening the box.

A new pipe and tin of tobacco were inside. Pleased, he withdrew the pipe.

Near sunset, they made camp. They built a fire, put on supper, and then tended to the horses.

"How far to the tracks?" Reeves said.

"Midday tomorrow," Joseph Walking Stick said.

As they ate supper, Reeves said, "What was in the box you gave Two Crows?"

"A new pipe and a tin of tobacco I picked up in Fort Smith before we left," Tillman said. "I didn't get the chance to break it in, so I thought he could enjoy it."

Reeves grinned. "Next time you visit, he might make you a member of the tribe."

"Joseph Walking Stick, have you a sweet tooth?" Tillman said.

"What do you have?" Joseph Walking Stick said.

"Canned peaches in sweet syrup," Tillman said.

"In that case, I have a sweet tooth," Joseph Walking Stick said.

From his horse, Tillman watched Reeves and Joseph Walking Stick inspect the tracks on the ground.

"Two weeks old and headed west," Reeves

said. "Six riders."

"Joseph Walking Stick, it was a pleasure riding with you," Tillman said. "But it's time for you to go home."

"I can't," Joseph Walking Stick said. "Two Crows told me to stay with you until these men are found. If I return now, he will know I left you, and he will be angry with me."

Reeves looked at Tillman. "Two Crows will be mad," he said.

Tillman sighed. "All right, but I make the calls," he said.

Three days later, Tillman, Reeves, and Joseph Walking Stick peered over the edge of a cliff at the camp of the Kincaid brothers. The six outlaws were having lunch and lying about.

Tillman motioned with his hand, and they all backed up to their horses.

"They're probably waiting for the smoke to clear before they move out," Tillman said.

"Looks like they've been settled in for a week now," Reeves said.

"Joseph Walking Stick, do you think you can find us a way down there before sunset?" Tillman said.

Joseph Walking Stick nodded.

"Go. Supper will be ready when you return," Tillman said.

■ ■ ■ ■

As they ate supper around a campfire, Tillman said, "How long will it take to reach them?"

"Two hours," Joseph Walking Stick said.

"How do you want to handle it?" Reeves said.

"Well, they are white men and outlaws," Tillman said. "That makes them stupid as well as lazy. What we'll do is, we'll just invite ourselves to breakfast."

"Breakfast?" Reeves said.

"Marshal Reeves, remember this one thing," Tillman said. "Your most powerful weapon against outlaws is always going to be the element of surprise."

Tillman, Reeves, and Joseph Walking Stick left the horses a hundred yards from the outlaws' camp and walked to them just before sunup.

Reeves and Joseph Walking Stick carried rifles. Tillman took only his Colt Peacemaker.

Ten feet from the sleeping outlaws, Tillman nodded, and Reeves and Joseph Walking Stick cocked the levers of their rifles.

Tillman drew his Colt, cocked it, and fired

a shot in the air.

Immediately the six outlaws bolted awake.

"Twitch, burp, or pass gas, and you're dead men," Tillman said. "Now, which two are the Kincaid brothers?"

One outlaw reached for his gun and Tillman shot him in the chest. A second outlaw reached for a rifle and Tillman put a hole in his shoulder.

"Are you deaf? Are you stupid? Or both?" Tillman shouted. "Now all of you, stand up slow and drop all weapons."

Five of the men stood and dropped their gun belts. The man with the chest wound couldn't stand.

"Bass, get the rope and tie them up. Then we'll tend to that man's wound," Tillman said.

"No," one of them men said. "I won't be hog-tied by no stinking darkie."

"You'll do as I say, or you'll never do anything again," Tillman said.

"No darkie puts his hands on me," the man said. "No stinking Indian savage neither."

"Fine," Tillman said. He stepped forward and knocked the man unconscious by smacking him across the jaw with his Colt. "Now, does anybody else wish to complain about the skin color of my two associates?"

■ ■ ■ ■

Joseph Walking Stick guarded the five prisoners while Tillman and Reeves removed the bullet from the wounded outlaw's chest.

"Think he'll make it?" Reeves said.

"He'll make it if we let him rest a few days," Tillman said. "Now let's tend to the other one with the shoulder wound."

After they patched up the second wounded outlaw, Tillman said, "Well, Bass, this is your country. Any ideas about a shortcut back to Fort Smith. I don't fancy two weeks in the saddle wet-nursing these men."

"We're a day and a half ride from Tulsa," Reeves said. "We can take the railroad back to Fort Smith and save two weeks' saddle time."

"That's a fine idea," Tillman said. "What do you say, Joseph Walking Stick?"

"Will they let me ride the train?" Joseph Walking Stick said.

"You'll ride the train, by God," Tillman said. "You'll ride."

"That's Tulsa in the distance," Reeves said.

"Hold the line a moment," Tillman said.

Reeves stopped his horse, and the six

tethered outlaw horses behind him held up.

Tillman dismounted. "Joseph Walking Stick, step down for minute," he said.

As Joseph Walking Stick dismounted, Tillman dug a deputy's badge out of a saddlebag. "I am authorized to deputize men in time of need to act as deputy marshals," he said. "This is a time of need. Raise your right hand."

Joseph Walking Stick held up his right hand.

"I authorize you as a temporary deputy marshal. Say I swear," Tillman said.

"I swear," Joseph Walking Stick said.

"Pin this to your shirt," Tillman said.

Grinning, Joseph Walking Stick took the badge.

In Tulsa, Tillman used his federal authority to secure the last car on the train for the prisoners, Reeves, and Joseph Walking Stick.

The ride to Fort Smith took just eight hours.

Half the town lined the streets, from the railroad station to the courthouse, when they marched the six prisoners to the holding jail.

A trial was held. All six men were found guilty of bank robbery and murder.

A week after the trial, all six outlaws were

hung, and Judge Parker's reputation as the Hanging Judge was born.

CHAPTER SIXTEEN

Fort Smith, Arkansas, 1901

Reeves and Whitson met Tillman for breakfast in the restaurant in the lobby of the Piccadilly Hotel.

"This is a fine establishment," Tillman said as he sliced into a fried egg. "Last night I asked the desk clerk if they could brush my coat and launder a few shirts, and he told me they have this new washing method called dry cleaning. Ever hear of it?"

"It's been around about a year now," Whitson said. "It's some kind of process for cleaning clothes that uses chemicals. Stinks to high heaven."

"My train doesn't leave until two this afternoon. Feel like taking a ride to the country with me?" Tillman said.

Reeves looked at Whitson. "We got nothing pressing," he said.

"Well, maybe a little ride to the country will do us some good," Whitson said.

"We'll get our horses and meet you here after breakfast," Reeves said.

Just a few miles west of Fort Smith, the countryside wasn't much different from when Tillman first stayed there twenty-five years earlier.

The three men dismounted at a small creek that ran off the Arkansas River.

Tillman filled his pipe, lit the bowl, and they sat in the shade of a tall tree.

"Sam, what's it like up there in Montana?" Reeves said.

"Almost exactly like when I first started to build the ranch twenty years ago," Tillman said. "Not many people, for sure. It's still wide open for the most part. But it's cattle country, and cattle need lots of room. It keeps the population down, and we like it that way."

"Is that what you plan to do after you retire, be a full-time rancher?" Whitson said.

"Me and my sons," Tillman said. "And the both of you are welcome any time you have a mind to visit."

"Long cold winters that far north," Whitson said.

"No denying that," Tillman said. "But the most beautiful spring and summer you've ever seen, and a night sky as big as heaven itself."

"Hell, Sam, you should have been a poet," Whitson said.

"And miss being shot six times?" Tillman said. "So how is this new judge working out for you?"

"He's no Judge Parker, that's for sure," Whitson said.

"Hell, who is?" Tillman said. "Hard to believe he's been gone five years already."

"Yeah," Reeves said.

Tillman puffed on his pipe and looked at the creek.

"Soon I expect we'll all join him, and a way of life will be gone forever," Tillman said.

Fort Smith, Arkansas, 1896
The air was chilled by March winds when Tillman stepped off the train in Fort Smith. As he walked Blue to the street, he noted the many changes in town since he last visited.

The courthouse was no longer the only brick and stone structure. The streets were wider, and there were more shops and stores and fewer saloons.

Women dressed more like women in Chicago and Boston, and the men wore suits and ties instead of work clothes.

Wagons and carriages filled the streets. Men on horseback were scarce.

Fort Smith was growing and becoming an important community.

Although the walk to the courthouse was just a few blocks, Tillman mounted the saddle and rode Blue to the courthouse corral.

People on the streets stared at him as he rode past.

At the courthouse, Tillman put Blue in the corral with several other horses. "I won't be long," Tillman said as he rubbed Blue's neck. "Play nice with the other kids."

Judge Parker had the look about him of a man whose time on earth was growing short.

As he filled two shot glasses with whiskey, Parker said, "I'm told I have but months left of my life. I won't see the new century, Sam, and that's a fact."

"What is it you got, Judge?" Tillman said.

"Something the doctors call Bright's disease," Parker said. "Simply put, my kidney is failing, and when it goes, I go with it."

"I can't tell you how sorry I am to hear this, Judge," Tillman said.

"It's out of my hands, Sam. So, what brings you to Fort Smith?" Parker said.

"Crawford Goldsby, otherwise known as Cherokee Bill," Tillman said. "He and his gang are holed up in Oklahoma in the Indian Nation. He's killed eight men so far. I'd like to borrow Bass, if you don't mind."

"He's a bad one, Goldsby," Parker said. "Take Bass and another man, and if you find Goldsby's gang, I want the pleasure of hanging them right here in Fort Smith."

"I already have warrants from the Justice Department, but go ahead and write me some local ones," Tillman said.

"I suggest you take Marshal Whitson along with Reeves," Parker said. "Whitson is a good man, and they're used to working together."

Tillman found Bass Reeves and Cal Whitson in the office reserved for district marshals on call.

They were having coffee at their desks, along with a few other marshals.

"Sam. Sam Tillman! Why didn't you telegram you were coming to town?" Reeves said as he shook hands with Tillman.

"Don't tell me you forgot everything I taught you about the element of surprise," Tillman said.

"It's the only rule I live by," Reeves said. "Sam, this is Cal Whitson."

Tillman and Whitson shook hands. "I've heard a great deal about you, Marshal," Whitson said.

"Some of it good, I hope," Tillman said.

"So, why are you here, Sam?" Reeves said.

"How's the coffee here?" Tillman said.

"Terrible," Reeves said.

"Is that little café still across the street?" Tillman said.

Tillman, Reeves, and Whitson sat at a table beside the window and sipped their coffee.

"Place hasn't changed in twenty years," Tillman said.

"And the food is just as bad," Reeves said.

"Have you heard of Crawford Goldsby?" Tillman said.

"Calls himself Cherokee Bill," Whitson said. "He's out of Judge Parker's jurisdiction, or we'd be out after him right now."

"He's hiding out in Oklahoma in the Indian Nation," Tillman said. "That's Parker's district. I have federal warrants for his arrest. I thought you'd care to accompany me, seeing as how the entire Indian Nation belongs to Parker, and Cherokee Bill is not out of my territory."

"I heard he's killed six people," Reeves said.

"Closer to nine," Tillman said.

"When do you want to leave?" Whitson said.

"First light," Tillman said. "But I'd like to make one stop along the way."

Tillman rented a sturdy mule for the trip and purchased a hundred pounds of food at the dry goods store for the mule to carry.

Tillman met Reeves and Whitson at the little café near the courthouse for breakfast. They had left for the Indian Nation by eight o'clock.

"Tell me, Bass, is that river raft still in operation?" Tillman said.

"It is, but there's been something of what you'd call modification," Reeves said.

"Modification?" Tillman said.

"You'll see," Whitson said.

By two in the afternoon, they reached the river crossing. The flat raft had been replaced by a wide riverboat with gates on each end. The ropes were gone and in their place were two steel cables.

The cables were attached to two large wheels in a diesel-powered combustion engine.

"A combustion engine. I'll be damned,"

Tillman said.

"It came from Germany," Whitson said. "Some man named Benz built it."

"It's five dollars to cross now, Sam," Reeves said. "Two dollars extra for the mule."

"Highway robbery," Tillman said. "But I don't fancy losing two days circling the Ozarks."

The old cabin had been replaced by a ranch-style home that also served as an office.

Tillman paid the seventeen dollars, and one man started the engine. When Tillman, Reeves, and Whitson had loaded the horses and mule, the man put the engine in gear, and the riverboat, piloted by the cables, took off across the river.

What used to take thirty minutes to cross the river now took just five. On the opposite shore, the riverboat stopped at a dock, and Tillman lowered the gate.

Once everyone was on land, the riverboat, powered by the diesel engine, returned to its home shore.

From there Tillman, Reeves, and Whitson rode to the center of the reservation and arrived shortly before nightfall. They rode directly to the cabin of Two Crows.

Joseph Walking Stick, in his late forties

now, was seated in a rocking chair on the front porch.

"Joseph Walking Stick, it's good to see you," Tillman said. "How is Two Crows?"

"The doctor is in with him," Joseph Walking Stick said. "Go in. He would like to see you."

Tillman, Reeves, and Whitson entered the cabin. The reservation doctor and his nurse were in the living room, having coffee.

"Marshal Reeves, Marshal Whitson. What are you doing here?" the doctor said.

"Passing through," Reeves said. "We thought we'd check on old Two Crows. How is he?"

"He's dying is how he is," the doctor said.

"From what?" Tillman said.

"From being eighty-nine and having the influenza," the doctor said.

"Can we see him?" Tillman said.

"Just for a minute," the doctor said. "He's very weak."

Reeves and Tillman opened the bedroom door and quietly entered. Two Crows was in bed, under a blanket. His eyes were closed, and his breathing was shallow.

"Two Crows, it's Bass Reeves," Reeves said. "I brought Sam Tillman with me. Can you hear me, Two Crows?"

Slowly, Two Crows opened his eyes and

looked at Reeves. "Reeves. It is good to see you again," he said. "Who is that with you?"

"It's Sam Tillman," Reeves said.

"Come closer. My eyes are not what they once were," Two Crows said.

"Hi, Two Crows," Tillman said as he approached the bed. "It gladdens my heart to see you again, old friend."

"Are you well?" Two Crows said.

"Yes," Tillman said.

"I am dying," Two Crows said.

"I know, and I am very glad I got this chance to tell you what a good friend you have always been to me," Tillman said.

"We will see each other again on the other side one day," Two Crows said. "I hurt. Can you get the doctor for me?"

Tillman, Reeves, Whitson, and Joseph Walking Stick sat in chairs on the porch. Hundreds of members of the tribe surrounded the cabin.

Hours passed.

The cabin door opened and the doctor stepped out. "He's gone," the doctor said. "He went peacefully, without pain."

Joseph Walking Stick stood up and left the porch to give the news to the people of the tribe.

"I'm glad we stayed to see Two Crows get the respect he deserved," Tillman said to Joseph Walking Stick. "But we have a bad outlaw who needs to be brought to justice."

"I will go with you to help track," Joseph Walking Stick said. "Who are you after?"

"Crawford Goldsby, known as Cherokee Bill," Tillman said.

"Cherokee Bill is not welcome on our land," Joseph Walking Stick. "I'll get my horse and gear and be ready in a few minutes."

"He'll go to the high ground where he feels comfortable," Joseph Walking Stick said.

"He's probably got a gang of six or more with him," Tillman said. "We might have to do some killing. Goldsby knows he'll hang for sure if he's captured, so they'll fight us all the way."

"When we reach higher ground, I'll scout for tracks," Joseph Walking Stick said.

"I'll go with you," Reeves said.

They rode until an hour before sunset. While Tillman and Whitson made camp, Joseph Walking Stick and Reeves scouted ahead.

"We have some fresh beef we need to use," Tillman said. "I'll get a stew going."

While the stew cooked and coffee boiled, Tillman and Whitson tended to their horses. Then they drank coffee and waited for Reeves and Joseph Walking Stick to return.

Tillman lit his pipe and watched as Whitson adjusted the eye patch covering his left eye.

"When did you lose it?" Tillman said.

"October of sixty-three," Whitson said. "I was with the 3rd Arkansas Cavalry. Shrapnel from a rebel rampart took it. Funny thing is, I didn't even feel it."

"How long have you been a marshal?"

"Since eighty-nine," Whitson said. "Who did you serve with?"

"Grant," Tillman said. "A few others, but mostly Grant."

"I think they're back," Whitson said.

As they ate bowls of beef stew with thick hunks of crusty bread, Reeves said, "We spotted a trail leading to high ground. We think it's them."

"How old?" Tillman said.

"A week, maybe ten days," Reeves said.

"And they'll stay put for a while, too," Tillman said. "Because they know the Texas Rangers, Oklahoma Marshals, and every local sheriff in three states are looking for them, so that gives us an advantage."

"How?" Joseph Walking Stick said.

Reeves smiled. "The element of surprise," he said.

Tillman set his bowl aside and filled his cup with coffee. He took out his pipe, but before he could fill it from his pouch, Joseph Walking Stick removed a small sack from his gear and handed it to Tillman.

"Two Crows asked me to give this to you," he said.

Tillman took the sack, opened it, and removed the pipe he had given Two Crows twenty years earlier.

"He told me to tell you thanks for the loan of a good smoke," Joseph Walking Stick said.

"Well, I'll be," Tillman said.

As good a tracker as Reeves was, he was no match for the skills of Joseph Walking Stick as they made their way into the higher ground of the Ozark Mountains.

At lower altitude, the temperatures were in the mid-sixties, but this high up snow was still on the ground, and they had to break out the much warmer overcoats from their gear.

They slept with a fire burning all night to keep the horses and mule warm.

After four days of hard riding, when they stopped to make lunch, Joseph Walking Stick scouted ahead.

He returned after an hour with news.

"Goldsby and his people are holed up in a cabin in a small box canyon on the other side of that ridge," he said and pointed northwest.

"Let's eat, and we'll go have a look," Tillman said.

The four men stood on the ledge overlooking the box canyon and studied the situation below. A fairly large cabin with smoke rising from a tin stove pipe had been built in the canyon. A corral with nine horses sat to its left. Behind the cabin stood an outhouse.

"Joseph Walking Stick, do you know who built this cabin?" Tillman said.

"No."

"I think I do," Reeves said. "Back in eighty-one, there was talk of a hermit who went into the mountains. Folks in town said he had two pack mules loaded with building tools and such, but nobody has seen him since."

"That's fifteen years ago," Whitson said. "More than enough time to build a cabin and corral."

"Joseph Walking Stick, do you think you can find us a way down there and be back before nightfall?" Tillman said.

Joseph Walking Stick nodded, walked to his horse, and mounted the saddle. "What's for supper?" he said.

While Joseph Walking Stick was away, they made camp several hundred yards away from the edge of the cliff so as not to be detected by Goldsby below.

Joseph Walking Stick returned a little before sunset.

"There is an easy way down an hour west of here," he said.

"How long of a ride would it be?" Tillman said.

"If we left at dawn, we'd be there in two hours," Joseph Walking Stick said.

"Grab a plate of food," Tillman said. "We'll be leaving early come morning."

They studied the cabin from behind some large rocks on a hill from a distance of about two hundred yards.

"What do you want to do, Sam?" Reeves said.

"No smoke in the chimney," Tillman said. "They're still sleeping off last night's liquor. Let's get back to the horses."

At the top of the hill, the horses were

tethered to a large tree.

"Joseph Walking Stick, break out your bow and six arrows," Tillman said. "Bass, Cal, grab your Winchesters."

Tillman removed a bottle of whiskey from a saddlebag along with a long-sleeved undershirt.

"Joseph Walking Stick, from what distance can you hit the cabin roof and front walls?" Tillman said.

"A hundred and fifty yards," Joseph Walking Stick said. "Maybe a bit more."

"Good enough," Tillman said.

The men returned to the hill and took a position behind large rocks about a hundred and fifty yards from the cabin.

Tillman used his field knife to cut strips from his undershirt and then wrapped each around the six arrows. Then he soaked each wrapped strip in whiskey.

"We'll give them a chance to surrender," Tillman said.

"If they don't?" Whitson said.

"Bass, wake them up with a shot through a window," Tillman said. "The rest is their choice."

Reeves cocked his Winchester and fired a shot through a glass window.

After a few seconds, Goldsby yelled out from inside the cabin. "Who all is out there?

Show yourself, you lousy coward."

"United States Marshal Sam Tillman and a posse," Tillman shouted. "We have you surrounded and cut off. Come out with your hands up and you won't get hurt. You have my word."

"The word of a law dog ain't worth spit," Goldsby shouted.

Tillman turned to Joseph Walking Stick and nodded. Joseph Walking Stick placed an arrow against his bowstring, and Tillman lit the whiskey-soaked strip with a match.

"Go ahead," Tillman said.

Joseph Walking Stick aimed and fired the arrow into the roof. After a few seconds, the dry wood caught fire.

Then, one by one, Joseph Walking Stick fired flaming arrows onto the cabin.

Within minutes, the entire roof and front wall were engulfed in flames. Thick smoke rose up from the growing flames.

"If they want to surrender when they come out, give them the opportunity," Tillman said. "If they decide to fight, shoot."

The fire spread quickly and soon the entire cabin was in flames. The front door opened, and the outlaws rushed out and collapsed to the ground.

"Drop all weapons and put your hands up," Tillman shouted. "Any man draws a weapon is a dead man. Test me at your own peril."

One of the outlaws attempted to run to the corral and Tillman shot him in the leg.

"Anyone else want to test my resolve?" Tillman shouted.

None of the outlaws moved.

"Well then," Tillman said.

They tied the nine outlaws with rope inside the corral.

"Why did you have to burn the cabin?" Goldsby said. "That was just a mean thing to do."

"So that others wanted by the law can't use it as a hideout," Tillman said.

The outlaw shot in the leg looked at Tillman. "You shot me. You had no call to do that, no call at all."

"I gave you fair warning," Tillman said. "So don't cry about the outcome."

"But I'm still bleeding," the outlaw said.

"We'll patch you up so you can ride," Tillman said.

"What for?" Goldsby said. "They just gonna hang us. Just let him die."

Tillman looked at Goldsby. "How old are you, son?" he said.

"Twenty," Goldsby said.

"You killed nine men, and you'll hang,

and you won't see your twenty-first birth-day," Tillman said. "And for what? Money that wasn't yours to begin with?"

"Screw you, law dog," Goldsby said. "You're a coward, or you'd'a fought me fair. You're no better than an Indian squaw."

Tillman grabbed Goldsby by his roped wrists and yanked him to his feet. He then pulled his field knife and cut Goldsby's ropes, then replaced the knife, removed his holster, and dropped it to the ground.

"All right, pup. Is your bite worse than your bark?" Tillman said.

Goldsby looked at Tillman.

"They're going to hang you, son," Tillman said. "Now is your chance to get some licks in before you go."

Goldsby screamed and charged Tillman. Tillman stepped to his right and tripped Goldsby with his left boot.

Tillman grabbed Goldsby by the shirt, yanked him to his feet, and then back-handed him several times with his right hand.

"I hate the thought of any man swinging from a rope," Tillman said, and he back-handed Goldsby several more times. "But you . . . it will be my pleasure to watch you choke your last breath."

Tillman backhanded Goldsby three more

times and then shoved him to the ground and picked up his holster.

"Best make peace with your maker while you have time," Tillman said and walked away.

Whitson grabbed another piece of rope and tied Goldsby's hands. "It doesn't pay to aggravate Sam Tillman, does it?" he said.

Three days later, they arrived in Tulsa, and from there they took the railroad to Fort Smith.

At one time, the citizens of Fort Smith were accustomed to seeing the outlaw wagon arrive packed with outlaws going to trial, but those wild days were long gone. So when Tillman, Reeves, Whitson, and Joseph Walking Stick escorted Goldsby and his gang from the railroad to the courthouse, people lined the streets as if watching a parade.

Tillman stayed to testify at the trial. Two weeks later, Goldsby and his gang were executed by hanging.

On March 17, 1896, Goldsby was walked to the gallows. A minister asked him if he had any final words.

Goldsby replied, "I came here to hang, not make a speech."

Six months later, Tillman returned to Fort

Smith to attend the funeral of Judge Isaac Parker.

Fort Smith, Arkansas, 1901
At the courthouse, Tillman shook hands with Reeves and Whitson.

"See you at your retirement party next month," Reeves said.

"You bet," Tillman said.

Tillman mounted Blue and decided to take a last ride to the street once known as Courthouse Way.

He stopped in front of a warehouse that had once been his home. He could see Mary Elizabeth planting her flowers in the front garden while his boys and the Reeves children played in the street with a kite.

Mary Elizabeth was in good health then and strong as a young bull.

They were supposed to grow old together and live out their days in Montana, surrounded by their children and grandchildren.

Along the way, the man upstairs had different plans for them, which took them on an entirely different path.

Life worked that way sometimes.

The element of surprise didn't apply only to fighting wars and catching outlaws.

Tillman took out his flask and said, "To

the good days of long ago."

He toasted Mary Elizabeth, tucked the flask away, and said, "Let's go, Blue."

When Tillman rode to the railroad station, he didn't notice Brass at the end of the platform.

CHAPTER SEVENTEEN

1901

Tillman sat beside a window and watched the scenery roll by at fifty-five miles an hour.

Old Blue, at his best, could manage thirty miles an hour and only for a short distance of about two miles.

The world had grown up and found itself in one big hurry.

Why, and to go where, were questions that went unanswered in Tillman's mind. The old west was gone and civilization had won out, as it always does. Soon it would exist only in the memories of old men like him and the dime novels featuring Wyatt Earp, Bat Masterson, and Calamity Jane.

As he looked out the window, Tillman allowed his mind to wander.

Tillman moved his family to Phoenix, Arizona, in the spring of seventy-nine. At the time, Phoenix was a small town of a thousand residents, and Arizona was decades away from statehood.

He settled his family into a nice home on the edge of town. Although the town and surrounding valley were flatlands, the mountains loomed in the distance.

At first the hot, arid climate seemed to help Mary Elizabeth's cough. She regained strength and stamina to the point where Tillman was able to travel overnight on official business.

When her health turned downhill, the end came quickly. The final two months of her life were spent drugged on morphine to ease her pain.

The day she died, Tillman held her hand, and she made him promise he would raise their boys to be strong, educated men.

He kept his promise and, with the help of Alice, reared his boys to become fine men.

At the time of Mary Elizabeth's death, they owned fifteen thousand acres of land in Montana. He sent the boys to stay with Alice while he took Mary Elizabeth's body by railroad to Miles City and then by wagon to their land.

He selected a shady spot under a large tree and dug the grave himself. In a few years, the back porch of the house he would build would face her headstone.

Tillman snapped out of his funk when the conductor came through to punch tickets.

"Is the dining car open yet?" Tillman said.

The conductor looked at his watch. "Ten minutes, sir," he said.

"Obliged," Tillman said. He took out his pocket watch, the watch given to him by his father, the very watch he'd carried throughout the Civil War and beyond. He gave it a few winds and then put it away.

He looked out the window again and then closed his eyes.

Shiloh, Tennessee, April 5th, 1862

Tillman was a young corporal in Grant's Army at the time. Grant had moved his troops deep into Tennessee, where they camped at Pittsburg Landing on the west bank of the Tennessee River.

Grant commanded a massive force of forty thousand men, but was taken by surprise the morning of April 6th, when Confederate General Beauregard led a surprise attack on Grant with forty thousand men, which was equal to the strength of Grant's Army.

Beauregard's objective was to drive Grant into the swamp, overwhelm his troops into submission, and deliver a crushing blow to the Union Army.

It was the first battle of the war for Tillman. He and thousands of others, including his friend since training, Glen Post, were embedded in a sunken road they called the Hornet's Nest when the surprise attack launched.

The war was still relatively young and most of Grant's soldiers, including Tillman, were inexperienced and had yet to shed blood.

Tillman, along with thousands of other untested soldiers, wondered how they would perform under battle conditions. Would they freeze? Would they cower in fear or run, or would they find courage, stand their ground, and fight?

Those questions were answered quickly when the first shots were fired.

Grant's artillery bombed the Confederates, the Confederates replied in kind, and the battle raged all day until nightfall.

Tillman had no idea how many men he killed that day, but he estimated between six and eight.

The battle continued the following morning. Aided by General Buell's troops of nearly eighteen thousand, the tide of the battle turned in Grant's favor.

When an officer fell dead from his horse, Tillman mounted the horse and rode with a cavalry charge at Confederate General Johnston's Army.

From horseback, Tillman killed another six men. His actions didn't go unnoticed.

By nightfall, Grant's Army emerged victorious.

The battle cost the lives of twenty-three thousand soldiers.

Tillman was promoted to sergeant and transferred to the cavalry division. There were a few minor skirmishes to deal with, but nothing like what was to come.

Vicksburg, Mississippi, 1863

In May of 1863, Grant moved his army across the Mississippi River to Vicksburg, the last major stronghold of the Confederate Army. He camped his seventy-seven thousand troops along the Mississippi River.

Grant's attack was against the army led by Confederate General John C. Pemberton. The siege lasted forty days. Casualties on the Confederate side were staggering.

After Grant captured the Mississippi capital of Jackson, Pemberton was forced to retreat westward.

Tillman, part of a large cavalry force, took part in the pivotal Battle of Champion Hill, a decisive victory for Grant that led to the surrender of Vicksburg. On his downtime,

Tillman took every opportunity to work with and train his horse to respond to certain commands. With practice, Tillman found he was a deadly shot from the saddle, and he used his skills in battle. He carried four Colt revolvers to cut down on reloading time in the saddle.

While Grant's Army attacked in waves, the cavalry protected the flanks and did considerable damage to Pemberton's army.

Tillman, an experienced horseman by this time, displayed superior skill in leading his men in the face of the enemy. From horseback, he felled a dozen or more Confederate soldiers.

On the forty-seventh day of the siege, on July 4, 1863, Pemberton surrendered the city of Vicksburg to Grant.

Before Grant's next major battle, Tillman was given a field promotion to lieutenant and a special assignment.

Tillman handpicked forty cavalry soldiers to command. The assignment was to push into enemy territory and do as much damage to supply lines and supply trains as possible in order to disrupt the Confederate Army's ability to resupply.

By September, Tillman and his horse soldiers were ready for their assignment. They left Grant's Army and took off on their own.

Riding deep into the south, starting in Mississippi, Tillman led his soldiers on several raids on railroad lines, destroying tracks and disrupting Confederate supply lines.

From Mississippi, Tillman led his men into Louisiana, where they destroyed several bridges key to Confederate movement.

They spent the new year of 1864 in Alabama, Tennessee, and Mississippi.

In Alabama, Tillman and his men destroyed a pivotal railroad bridge that was a key Confederate supply line. They also intercepted the battle and travel plans for several Confederate generals, and, using a portable telegraph box, were able to wire the plans to Grant.

Tillman moved his men into Tennessee in the spring. His scouts located about one hundred troops traveling in fifty wagons filled with ammunition, food, and medical supplies.

The wagons were a two-day ride to the west.

As Tillman's group camped for the night, Tillman told his men they needed to attack and stop those supply wagons at all costs.

"The war is all but won at this point, men," Tillman said. "We can't let the Confederate Army get those supplies and hold out longer than necessary. We're forty to their one hundred, but they're in wagons, and we will have the advantage of surprise."

Tillman and his forty men were armed with Burnside carbine rifles, one of the most advanced rifles of the day. It fired a self-contained .54 caliber cartridge accurate up to two hundred yards. This gave them a huge advantage over the one hundred Confederate soldiers driving the wagons.

"I want ten men on each flank, ten in the rear, and ten out front to cut off their escape," Tillman said. "Any Confederates who wish to surrender may do so. Any who wish to fight, kill them. We cannot allow these supply wagons to reach the Confederate Army."

Tillman selected a secluded spot on the road that gave good cover to his men and closed the front and back doors to the wagons' route.

The wagons rolled by around nine in the morning. Tillman gave his men in the flanks the order to attack.

Armed with the high-powered Burnside carbine rifles, the Confederate soldiers didn't stand a chance as Tillman's men picked them off like a carnival shooting booth. Some men tried to run, but the ten horse soldiers in front cut them down. Wagons in the rear tried to turn and run, and were cut down by the horse soldiers in the rear.

Forty Confederate soldiers were killed in the skirmish; sixty surrendered.

Tillman gave the sixty Confederate soldiers food, water, and some medical supplies, and sent them walking back to where they came from. Then he had his men take as much food, water, and medical supplies as they could carry. He gave orders to burn the rest, including the wagons.

Word of Tillman's attack on the supply wagons spread quickly, and Tillman had to travel to Alabama to escape the Confederate patrols sent to find him.

Forty miles west of Troy, Alabama, Tillman and his men encountered a Confederate patrol of fifty men.

Although Tillman's men had the advantage of the Burnside rifle, the battle in the woods lasted nearly four hours before the Confederates surrendered or retreated.

Tillman lost several of his men and took a bullet in his left leg. His men removed the bullet, but, wounded and weakened, Tillman headed for Kentucky, which had been under Union control since sixty-two.

He found a large farmhouse near Bowling

Green owned by a widow. There he was able to rest up for three weeks until he was well enough to ride again. While Tillman recovered, his men helped the widow by chopping wood, repairing fences, hunting game, and doing any odd jobs she needed done.

Once he was well enough to travel, Tillman led his horse soldiers north to Georgia, where they met up with Sherman's Army as it marched toward the sea unopposed, destroying everything in its path.

Sherman's Army captured Savannah in late December.

Tillman and his men were riding to join Grant's Army in April when word reached them that Lee surrendered to Grant on April 9, 1865.

Tillman and his men reached Grant the day President Lincoln was assassinated.

On May 9, the war officially ended.

1901

Tillman sipped coffee in the large dining car. He sat beside a window and smoked his pipe.

Outside the window, darkness had set in and there was nothing to see, but he always preferred a window, even at night.

Odd how memories from as far back as forty years ago could seem as if they happened just yesterday.

June 1865

Tillman was selected by Grant to serve as an officer in a military police unit during the reconstruction of the southern states.

He was given thirty days' leave before he had to report to Atlanta. He took the first train north to New York City, where he then caught a train to Wisconsin.

He didn't write Mary Elizabeth he was coming home. He wrote her often, but mail could take two or three months to reach its destination, so he didn't bother to post a letter.

The Big Woods hadn't changed much, if at all, in the four-plus years Tillman was gone. The trees were as thick as ever, the grass as green, the streams as clear as he remembered.

As he rode his horse through the woods and onto the road home, it was as if the war had never existed at all.

He paused beside a stream, smoked his pipe, and tried to gather his thoughts and think of what he was going to say to Mary Elizabeth after being gone four years. He was never a wordsmith to begin with, but after four years, he had no idea what to say to her.

Mary Elizabeth was just eighteen when he left for the war, and a great deal had happened since then.

In the four years he'd been gone, Tillman had taken many lives. He knew killing people changed a man, if not in appearance, then inside, where it counted most.

He wondered if Mary Elizabeth would sense a change in him. Women were perceptive in that way, while he was not.

Tillman's fears were laid to rest when he reached the family farm in the afternoon and found Mary Elizabeth and his father toiling in the fields.

She spotted him from a thousand feet away, dropped her hoe, and ran to him. Tillman raced his horse to her, jumped from the saddle, and grabbed her in his arms.

Mary Elizabeth had proved to be even more able-bodied than he believed and had toiled in the field side by side with his father the entire time Tillman was away.

She and Tillman's mother also worked in the Women's Soldier's Aid Society, raising money for medical supplies and food for the soldiers away from home.

Mary Elizabeth's hands were no longer pale and soft, and the sun had added creases around her eyes, but to Tillman she was more striking-looking than ever.

She didn't argue or complain when Tillman told her he had orders to report to Atlanta to provide security for the reconstruction of the devastated southern states.

Her two questions were: for how long, and could she go with him?

The answers to her questions were that he didn't know, but that he would find out and write her with the information.

They made the most of the twenty-six days they had together. In late July, Tillman left home to report to Atlanta.

Atlanta, Georgia, was once the crown jewel of the south, but after Sherman's March to the Sea, there wasn't much of it left standing. Sherman ordered the entire business district inside the city burned to the ground.

Before embarking on his March to the Sea, General Sherman ordered the complete destruction of Atlanta to prevent Confederates from recovering anything useful after he vacated the city.

Tillman served under General George Meade during his tenure in Georgia. In all, twenty thousand troops were deployed for the reconstruction of the south. The troops' purposes were to impose martial law and supervise local authorities.

Army engineers and building materials by the trainload were sent to the south, but the task of reconstruction was monumental.

The city, once home to ten thousand prosperous residents, was little more than a shell of its former self.

In addition to homelessness, poverty, and unemployment, there were now tens of thousands of freed slaves who had no idea how to live as a free people. In all, about four million freed slaves were scattered throughout the south.

Tillman learned quickly that theft would be a major concern. At night, men converged on the railroad depot and trains to steal valuable equipment and supplies. He tripled the number of guards and gave orders to shoot any man attempting to rob a train.

After dark, vandals would break into what stores there were and steal food, medicine, and clothing.

Murder and rape were also a problem. Tillman tolerated none of that sort of thing in his jurisdiction.

Those men who were caught suffered military justice, with imprisonment and, if warranted, execution by hanging or firing squad.

Tillman, under his present circumstances,

told Mary Elizabeth in a letter that conditions were not fit for her to join him.

The circumstances changed in late August, when General Grant came to Georgia.

Grant set up his headquarters in what was once a large plantation in the countryside south of Georgia.

Grant sent a rider to bring Tillman to the plantation.

Tillman met Grant in the large den, which he used as an office.

"At ease, Lieutenant," Grant said when Tillman was ushered into the den.

"You sent for me, General?" Tillman said.

"Yes," Grant said. "I was wondering when was the last time you were on a snipe hunt?"

"A snipe hunt, General?" Tillman said.

"My horse is standing by, Lieutenant," Grant said. "Let's go for a ride."

Accompanied by his protection detail of six soldiers, Grant led Tillman on a several-mile ride through the Georgia countryside.

"All this was once a large and prosperous plantation," Grant said. "Peanuts, pecans, corn, and blueberries. At one time, three hundred slaves worked this land. No man should ever be the property of another man. That looks like a good spot there under that pecan tree."

Grant and Tillman dismounted under the tall, wide tree and sat in the shade. The six soldiers stayed out of listening range and sat under another pecan tree.

Grant reached into his jacket and produced a pint bottle of bourbon whiskey. "Let the snipe hunt begin," he said.

Grant took a sip of whiskey and passed the bottle to Tillman.

Tillman took a sip and returned the bottle to Grant.

"President Johnson has approved the completion of the transcontinental railroad project that was halted by the war," Grant said. "It's estimated the project will take four years to complete. Chinese, Irish, and freed slaves will compose most of the workforce. In charge of the project is railroad builder and vice president of the Union Pacific Railroad, Thomas Durant. They call him Doc, because he actually went to medical school."

Grant paused to take another sip of whiskey.

"The project is scheduled to start in Omaha and proceed westward according to routes planned by Durant and his team of engineers," Grant said.

He passed the bottle to Tillman, who took a sip.

"Any questions?" Grant said.

"Yes, General, I was wondering why you are telling me all this?" Tillman said.

Grant grasped the bottle, took a sip, and said, "I want you to head the security detail for the project."

"Security detail?" Tillman said.

"You'll keep your rank of lieutenant, and also wear the title of chief of railroad police," Grant said. "You'll command twenty soldiers to act as peacekeepers. Your duties will include keeping the peace among the workers, fighting off Indians and anyone else who might be tempted to rob the railroad."

"General, my wife is . . ." Tillman said.

"You will have a private car to yourself," Grant said. "The workers will have tents and cots, but Durant, his engineers, and you will have a private car. Your compensation will be ten times what you could make in a year as a farmer."

Grant took another sip of whiskey and gave the bottle to Tillman.

"Who do I report to?" Tillman said.

"On railroad matters, to Durant. On security and police matters, to no one but myself," Grant said. "You'll have to rely mostly on your experience and your own good judgment."

Tillman sipped from the bottle. "When do I report to Omaha?"

"Is two weeks enough time to travel home for your wife?" Grant said.

"More than enough, General," Tillman said.

"Then I shall see you in Omaha in two weeks," Grant said.

Grant took the bottle, emptied it, and tossed it aside.

"Our snipe hunt has concluded," he said. "Lunch should be ready right about now if you'd care to join me."

"Omaha? Four years?" Mary Elizabeth said. "For God's sake, Sam."

"The starting point is Omaha," Tillman said. "We'll be traveling west through Wyoming Territory and beyond. This is our chance, Mary. I can make three, four thousand dollars a year for at least four years. We can start buying up our land in Montana for a ranch, a real ranch like we talked about."

"What will we live in while they build the railroad?" Mary Elizabeth said.

"General Grant has promised us our own railroad car," Tillman said.

"Three or four thousand a year?" Mary Elizabeth said. "How much land can we buy with that?"

"At twelve dollars an acre, a lot," Tillman said.

"It sounds like a dangerous job, Sam," Mary Elizabeth said.

"Not as dangerous as riding a horse into enemy fire during the last four years," Tillman said.

"That was a silly comment, wasn't it?" Mary Elizabeth said.

"If you say no, I'll turn it down and resign my position with the army," Tillman said.

"On your army pay and what we can raise on the farm, we'll be a hundred years old before we get our ranch," Mary Elizabeth said. "What should I bring?"

"Anything you want," Tillman said. "We can shop for some new clothes in Omaha."

"I've never been out of Wisconsin, Sam," Mary Elizabeth said.

"It's about time you travel, then," Tillman said.

"What if . . . what if I get pregnant?"

"Then we have us a baby," Tillman said.

Mary Elizabeth sighed. "Come help me pack," she said.

1901

The waiter in the dining car came to Tillman's table and filled his empty cup.

"Obliged," Tillman said.

He emptied the ashes from his pipe into the ashtray on the table and then filled the bowl with fresh tobacco. He struck a match and lit the pipe.

At the end of the dining car, Brass quietly sat at a table and drew a sketch of Tillman in his notepad.

When Tillman finished his coffee and stood up, Brass stood and left the dining car before Tillman could see him.

As he left the dining car, Tillman paused at the waiter's station.

"What time do we reach Washington?" Tillman said.

"Eight in the morning," the waiter said.

"Obliged," Tillman said.

CHAPTER EIGHTEEN

1901

Tillman led Blue off the train platform to the street. The station was about a mile from the White House, and Tillman figured Blue could stand to stretch his legs a bit.

He mounted the saddle and rode Blue east a bit of the tracks, then headed north and rode for several miles until he reached a pasture of sweet grass.

"It doesn't take much to lose civilization, does it, boy?" Tillman said and dismounted. "Even in 1901."

He let Blue eat his fill of sweet grass and sat under a tree in the shade.

He took out his pipe and lit a bowl. The morning air was mild with the promise of a beautiful spring day to come in Washington.

Tillman watched Blue munch grass. The massive horse could eat grass all day and never seem to get his fill.

"Well, Blue, in three weeks we both can

retire," Tillman said.

Blue turned his head and looked at Tillman.

"I always thought she'd be by my side on the day I handed in my badge," Tillman said. "But no man can see his future. All we can do is accept our fate for what it is."

Tillman felt a tear in his eye and he smiled at Blue. "She's been gone twenty years, and I still miss her every day of my life."

Sensing Tillman's sadness, Blue stopped eating grass and walked over to him.

"I guess you're right. It's time to get going," Tillman said.

After placing Blue in a livery near the White House, Tillman walked to the small park across the street from the vice president's office on Capitol Hill.

He found a vacant bench and took a seat.

The sun was warm, and he loosened the tie around his neck. He always hated wearing a tie and only did so when the occasion merited it.

Tillman took out his pipe and lit a fresh bowl of tobacco. Several horse-drawn carriages rolled by the park.

"Old friend or not, it's too nice a morning to rush indoors," he said.

■ ■ ■ ■

Omaha, Nebraska, 1865
Mary Elizabeth's first train ride was spent looking out the window at the scenery as it passed by at fifty-five miles an hour.

To her, traveling at such a dizzying speed was a breathtaking experience.

Tillman, on the other hand, spent most of the trip dozing, smoking his pipe, or reading a newspaper.

When they reached Omaha, Mary Elizabeth had never seen so big a town. Fifteen thousand residents, and every one of them appeared to be in a hurry.

Shops and stores seemed to be everywhere as they walked his horse to a livery near the railroad depot.

"What about our bags, Sam?" Mary Elizabeth said.

"A man is bringing them to our hotel," Tillman said.

"There are stores just for women," Mary Elizabeth said.

In Wisconsin, she occasionally shopped at the general store in town, so seeing a store just for women was a bit of a surprise.

"Yes, there are, and we'll visit one so you can pick out some new clothes as soon as we board my horse."

After boarding his horse, Tillman and Mary Elizabeth shopped at a women's clothing store, where they bought her two new outfits to wear at dinner. Mary Elizabeth fussed about spending forty dollars on just two dresses, but Tillman told her it was money well spent, and she conceded.

"After we check in at the hotel, we're meeting General Grant for dinner at seven o'clock," Tillman said.

"General Grant is having dinner with us?" Mary Elizabeth said.

"It's more like we're having dinner with him," Tillman said.

At the Hotel Omaha, Mary Elizabeth felt giddy just walking into so large and ornate a lobby.

When they checked into their room on the fourth floor, Mary Elizabeth was shocked at so large and lavish a room. The bed was twice the size of the bed they had back home.

Their bags were stacked neatly against a wall.

"We have time for a bath before we meet the general," Tillman said.

"A bath? Where?" Mary Elizabeth said.

"You expect me to take off my clothes in

here? What if somebody walks in on us?" Mary Elizabeth said.

"This is a private, reserved bathroom, honey," Tillman said. "I've got a key to lock the door, so go ahead and get undressed before the water gets cold."

Mary Elizabeth looked at the very large tub.

"There's only one tub," she said.

"That," Tillman said as he locked the door, "is the general idea."

Grant reserved the private dining hall for just the three of them. Even Grant's protection detail had to wait in the hallway.

Mary Elizabeth wore one of the new dresses they'd bought earlier and took special care with her hair.

Tillman wore his frock coat, white shirt, and a tie.

As they walked from their room to the private dining hall, Mary Elizabeth paused suddenly in a hallway.

"What?" Tillman said.

"I just realized I am going to meet General Grant and have dinner with him," Mary Elizabeth said.

"Where did you think we were going?" Tillman said.

"I knew where we were going, but . . . it's

General Grant," Mary Elizabeth said. "The most famous general of the war. What do I say to him?"

" 'Good evening' will do nicely," Tillman said.

"I'm serious, Sam," Mary Elizabeth said. "My first time ever out of Wisconsin, and we're having dinner with the most famous general of the war. Next to Lincoln, the most famous man in the whole country."

"Would you relax?" Tillman said. "He's a general and he's famous, for sure, but he's also not much different from anybody else."

"What do I say to him?" Mary Elizabeth said.

"Ask him about our snipe hunt," Tillman said.

"What's a snipe hunt?" Mary Elizabeth said.

Grant proved to be a charmer in a social situation, and Mary Elizabeth was immediately at ease at the dinner table.

Dinner was steak and baked chicken. Grant loved champagne, and a chilled bottle was served with the meal.

Grant asked about life in Wisconsin and seemed genuinely interested in Mary Elizabeth's stories about the Big Woods.

"Your husband is one of the finest soldiers

I've ever served with," Grant said. "He did a most dangerous job without question, and is probably responsible for a hundred confirmed kills in battle. You should be very proud of him."

Mary Elizabeth's face went pale for a moment as she looked at Tillman.

"He doesn't talk about the war much," she said.

"No, he's the kind who wouldn't," Grant said. "A trait I admire in a man. Sam, could you ask the desk to bring us another bottle of champagne?"

"Certainly," Tillman said and excused himself from the table.

"I see my remark upset you, and I do apologize," Grant said.

"No, General. I should apologize for acting like a schoolgirl," Mary Elizabeth said. "My husband spent four years in the war; it shouldn't come as a surprise to me that he killed men in battle."

"Sam is the best I've seen on the back of a horse," Grant said. "I entrusted him with the task of taking forty men deep into enemy territory and acting alone to disrupt Confederate supply lines, destroy bridges and railroad lines. His brilliance as a soldier is why I selected him for the task of protecting the railroad expansion west. If ever there was a horse soldier, it's your husband."

"I've never heard the term 'horse soldier' before, General," Mary Elizabeth said.

The door opened, and Tillman returned with a fresh bottle of champagne.

"Open the bottle, Sam, and let's drink a toast to the success of the railroad," Grant said.

"Sam, where are you?" Mary Elizabeth said.

"Right next to you, honey," Tillman said.

"This bed is too big," Mary Elizabeth said. "If everyone had a bed this big, no woman would even get pregnant. Turn on the lamp, please."

Tillman sat up and felt around on the nightstand for a match, lit it, and then lit the lantern.

"Now what is it, honey?" he said.

Mary Elizabeth sat up in bed and looked at Tillman. "When you went for more champagne . . . which tastes like vinegar with bubbles, by the way. Why would General Grant drink such terrible stuff?"

Tillman sighed. "I assume you have a question in there somewhere," he said.

"Yes. When you left to get another bottle, General Grant called you a horse soldier," Mary Elizabeth said. "Why haven't you ever told me about the things you did in the war?"

"It's best to let bad memories rest, honey," Tillman said. "I'd rather think about our future and what's ahead of us, rather than what's behind us."

Mary Elizabeth nodded. "I'd like two of each," she said and rested her head on the pillow.

"Two of each what?" Tillman said.

"Boys and girls."

"Oh."

"Turn out the light, Sam," Mary Elizabeth said. "The bed is getting cold."

"I feel silly having breakfast in my nightgown, Sam," Mary Elizabeth said.

"Best enjoy the comforts while we can, honey," Tillman said. "A lot of the road ahead is going to be bumpy."

"What should I do while you're at this meeting?" Mary Elizabeth said.

"Whatever you want," Tillman said. "Walk around town, see the sights, go shopping. I'm sure I'll be a while."

"I'd like to find a church," Mary Elizabeth said.

The meeting took place in the boardroom of the hotel. General Grant presided over the meeting. He introduced Thomas Durant as the project manager, General John Casement as chief engineer, and Tillman as chief of railroad police.

About twenty other investors and government officials were at the meeting. They all crowded around a long table where a large, very detailed map was centered.

"Gentlemen, it has taken years to plan this project," Durant said. "To connect east and west by railroad is a monumental feat that will change the lives of every American. What now takes months will eventually take seven days."

Durant used a pointer and tapped Omaha on the map.

"Our starting point is here," he said. "We will progress westward through Wyoming and into Utah, where we will join with the Central Pacific and form one transcontinental railroad."

Durant pointed to Salt Lake City in Utah.

"Somewhere around here we will connect." Durant said. "Every day of this journey will be documented for the ages. Every plan, every detail has been gone over for months, and we are ready. The workers are ready, General Casement is ready, and I am ready. The work begins tomorrow."

"Mr. Durant and I will take questions

now," Grant said.

The meeting lasted until two in the afternoon. Durant explained how the entire operation would travel by train. Men, equipment, food, supplies, everything would be housed on a twenty-car-long train.

The goal was between three and five miles a day of new track. Casement and his team of engineers would scout ahead to plan the best routes to take westward.

Durant wanted two hundred and fifty miles of new track laid before the onset of deep winter and, if winter was mild, to keep going as far as possible.

Entire towns consisting of tents would be constructed and moved every twenty miles. Supplies would be replenished as needed by a secondary supply train and moved by wagons.

Protection for the operation would be supplied by Tillman and his squad of twenty railroad police.

"Tomorrow morning, Mr. Durant, General Casement, Sam Tillman and I, and members of Congress will meet at the railroad yard to take an initial inventory of supplies and men. After that, we will decide if any last-minute additions are necessary," Grant said. "I have a banquet dinner planned for tonight, and all are invited.

Seven o'clock in the banquet hall."

Washington, D.C., 1901
Tillman emptied the spent tobacco from his pipe, stood up from the bench, crossed the street, and walked to the office of the vice president on Capitol Hill.

As soon as Tillman entered the lobby of the building, Brass emerged from the park and looked at the building.

He sat on the same bench as Tillman had occupied and took out his notepad.

CHAPTER NINETEEN

Washington, D.C., 1901
Vice President Theodore Roosevelt stood in the gardens behind his office. With him were two aids. Roosevelt turned to his aids, and one of them handed him a big game shotgun.

"Shells," Roosevelt said.

"But Mr. Vice President," an aide said.

"Shells, damn you," Roosevelt said.

The aid handed Roosevelt two massive, 6-gauge shells. Roosevelt opened the breech, loaded the two shells, and snapped it closed.

"Now stand back," Roosevelt said as he took aim at a young tree.

"Mr. Vice President, we've had to replant that tree twice this month already," the aide said.

Roosevelt fired the shotgun, and the enormous blast cut the tree in half.

"Well, that's all right. Let me have the British rifle," Roosevelt said.

The aide took the shotgun and handed Roosevelt a .303 British rifle called the Lee-Metford.

"Magazine," Roosevelt said.

The aide handed Roosevelt a ten-round magazine.

Roosevelt loaded the magazine into the rifle and proceeded to fire ten rounds into what was left of the tree, reducing it to splinters.

"Splendid, splendid. I have a notion to try some of those new hand grenades the army has designed," Roosevelt said.

"Mr. Vice President, please," an aide said. "No hand grenades."

"All right, all right. Give me the new carbine," Roosevelt said.

"Mr. Vice President, the Secretary of Agriculture has been waiting in your office for ten minutes," another aide said.

"What does that popinjay want?" Roosevelt said.

"He has an appointment, sir."

"Damn."

"Shall I contact the greenhouse and have a new tree delivered?" the aide said.

"Tell them we need a larger tree. I'm tired of shooting at splinters," Roosevelt said.

"Yes, Mr. Vice President," the aide said.

■ ■ ■ ■

At his desk, Roosevelt appeared bored to tears as he listened to the Secretary of Agriculture talk about some project or another. Truth be told, Roosevelt wasn't listening to one word of his dribble.

A knock sounded on the door.

"Yes," Roosevelt said.

The door opened and an aide stepped in.

"There is a United States Marshal here to see you Mr. Vice President," the aide said.

"Does he have an appointment?" Roosevelt said.

"No sir," the aide said.

"Well, what's his name?" Roosevelt said.

"Tillman. Sam Tillman," the aide said.

"Why the hell didn't you say so? Send him in," Roosevelt snapped as he jumped to his feet.

Roosevelt looked at the Secretary of Agriculture. "You, out," Roosevelt said.

"But Mr. Vice President, our appointment," the Secretary of Agriculture said.

"Later. Out."

Roosevelt and Tillman walked in the garden behind Roosevelt's office. A team of secret service agents followed closely behind them.

201

Roosevelt turned and looked at the agents.

"Would you men get out of here," Roosevelt snapped. "This man is one of my oldest friends."

"He has a gun, sir," an agent said.

"Of course he's carrying a gun, you idiot," Roosevelt said. "He's a United States Marshal. What did you think he was going to carry, a slingshot?"

"It's all right, Ted," Tillman said.

Tillman slowly withdrew his Colt and tossed it to the agent.

"I'll pick it up on the way out," Tillman said.

The agent nodded and stepped backward.

"How have you been, Sam?" Roosevelt said.

"Fine, and you?"

"Cut the horseshit, Sam. We've known each other too long for such idle chitchat," Roosevelt said.

"I'm retiring in a few weeks, Ted," Tillman said.

"Well, hell, I know that. Your man Post arranged a party. I'm the guest speaker. Seth Bullock will be there, too," Roosevelt said.

"I'm not sure how I feel about the whole thing. I'll be a full-time rancher, and I've never been anything but a full-time lawman before," Tillman said.

"Hell, Sam, do you think I started out to be vice president? Shit just happens to a man along the way." Roosevelt said. "You should know that better than anybody. You've done your duty a hundred times over; it's time to do for yourself now."

"Before I forget, how is old Seth these days?" Tillman said.

"Fine, just fine. I never did get the chance to thank you properly for teaching my Rough Riders the fine art of horse soldiering before we left for Cuba. Me, too, for that matter," Roosevelt said.

"Seth did his share, as I recall," Tillman said.

"Seth Bullock is a great lawman, for sure, but he's no horse soldier," Roosevelt said.

"I'm just sorry I couldn't go with you to Cuba. The boss wouldn't let me," Tillman said.

"I know that. But what you taught us went with us and made the difference, so in a way you were with us, Sam," Roosevelt said.

Tillman looked at the splintered remains of the tree.

"Still experimenting with new weapons, I see," Tillman said.

"Modern times, Sam. There's a telephone installed in a room somewhere in the White House, although there is no one to call. It never rings. But one day it will," Roosevelt said. "And the day it starts ringing, it will never stop."

"Walking over here from the train, I saw a horseless carriage. It was just parked at the curb. Some kids were looking at it," Tillman said.

"Someday, Sam, it will be the other way around, and the kids will be looking at the horse as a novelty." Roosevelt said.

With a hint of sadness in his eyes, Tillman nodded his agreement. "I expect you are right on that account," he said.

"How long has it been since the Little Missouri River?" Roosevelt said.

"Fifteen, sixteen years at least," Tillman said.

"Has it been that long?" Roosevelt said.

"A lot has happened since then, Mr. Vice President," Tillman said.

"Oh, stop with the vice president bullshit. So what are you doing in Washington if you're retirement isn't for weeks, Sam?" Roosevelt said.

"Passing through on a final assignment," Tillman said.

"You're a bad liar, Sam," Roosevelt said. "Listen, come to dinner tonight. Stay overnight. You can do your final assignment tomorrow."

"I don't want to put anybody out," Tillman said.

"Oh, for God's sake, Sam," Roosevelt
said. "Come on."

They returned to Roosevelt's office, where
he wrote his address on a slip of paper.

"Seven o'clock sharp, and bring your gear.
You're staying overnight," Roosevelt said.
"And no isn't an option."

"All right, Ted," Tillman said.

"I'll walk you out."

On the front steps, Tillman and Roosevelt
shook hands. Roosevelt held Tillman's Colt
and returned it to him.

"That's one beautiful piece," Roosevelt
said.

Tillman placed the Colt into the holster,
nodded, and started down the steps. He
paused and looked back to Roosevelt.

"Tell me something, Ted. Any ideas about
running for president?" Tillman said.

"Heaven forbid. It would interfere with
my plans to big game hunt in Africa," Roosevelt said.

"Well, if you do decide to run, you can
count on my vote," Tillman said.

"Count on coming with Seth and me on a
hunt in Africa," Roosevelt said.

Tillman nodded. "See you tonight," he
said.

"Don't be late," Roosevelt said. "Edith hates it when people are late."

Tillman nodded and walked down the steps to the sidewalk. He turned to his right and walked past the park.

In the park, on the bench, Brass watched Tillman walk by and then looked at Roosevelt, still standing on the steps.

In his notebook, Brass sketched a picture of Tillman and Roosevelt shaking hands.

Tillman walked to the livery and went in to get his gear and Winchester rifle.

"I'm leaving my horse until tomorrow," Tillman told the livery manager. "Do you have a place I can store my Winchester until the morning?"

"We have a gun safe in the office," the livery manager said. "Cost you an extra buck."

"Put it all on my bill," Tillman said.

Tillman left the livery and had several hours to kill. He walked to Capitol Hill and found a small café overlooking the railroad depot.

Of all things, they had tables on the street, like in Omaha.

Tillman ordered a large coffee, sat at a table on the sidewalk, smoked his pipe, and watched the railroad in the distance.

Chapter Twenty

Omaha, 1865

When Tillman told Mary Elizabeth about the banquet dinner at the hotel at seven o'clock that evening, she all but panicked.

"Sam Tillman, you know very well I've never attended such an affair before," she said. "What do I wear? What do I say? Will there be music and dancing?"

"You're asking the wrong person, honey," Tillman said. "We didn't exactly have a formal calendar of events back in the Big Woods, and I was too busy trying to stay alive during the war to attend many cotillions."

Mary Elizabeth sat on the small dressing bench in front of the dresser.

"Oh, God, I'm sorry, Sam," she said. "Sometimes I forget how terrible the war must have been for you."

"Don't worry a hair on your pretty head about that, honey," Tillman said. "We have time to go shopping for tonight. I'm sure the lady at the women's store can advise you on what dress to buy. Also, my only formal jacket is the one I married you in."

"You look so handsome in that new jacket, Sam," Mary Elizabeth said as they entered the banquet hall.

"And you look prettier than any other woman in the room," Tillman said.

Mary Elizabeth blushed as a waiter showed them to Grant's table. At the table were Durant and his wife, Hannah; General Casement and his wife, Marion; and a few investors and their wives.

Grant made the introductions, then left the table to take the stage and make a short speech before dinner was served.

Dinner consisted of two courses. Steak, chicken, and champagne were served at every table.

In the corner of the hall, a three-piece band played soft music so people's conversations weren't muffled.

Dessert was a cake in the shape of a railroad engine car running across tracks. Durant cut the ceremonial first piece. After everyone was served cake and coffee, Durant took the stage and made a speech.

By ten o'clock, the festivities had ended.

"Mrs. Tillman, may I borrow your husband for a bit?" Grant said to Mary Elizabeth. "I promise to have him back within the hour."

"Certainly, General," Mary Elizabeth said.

"Go on back to the room, honey," Tillman said. "I'll join you shortly."

"Let's go to my room," Grant said.

Grant's room was actually a suite with a bedroom, living room, and den. The den had a well-stocked bar.

"Pour us a couple of bourbons, will you, Sam?" Grant said as he removed his jacket and tie.

At the bar, Tillman poured two ounces of bourbon into two glasses and handed one glass to Grant.

"Let's sit," Grant said.

They took seats on the sofa. Grant lit a cigar, Tillman his pipe.

"This task you are about to undertake, it's not going to be easy," Grant said. "You're going to have hostile Indians, thieves, and the entire operation under your protection. The summer is going to be hot, and the winters, cold. Casement is a good man. He knows his stuff. Durant is a bit of a blowhard, but I don't expect you to have much trouble out of him. You're committing to four years at least, Sam. That's a big chunk for any man to bite off."

"General, I just spent four years in the war," Tillman said. "The next four years is going to pay a lot better. Besides, my wife and I have plans to buy our own land in Montana with the money I'll make, so don't worry about the commitment. I do have one small request, though."

"Ask," Grant said.

"The twenty men assigned to me are all army men," Tillman said. "I'd like one of them to be Glen Post. We served together, and he's a good man. Can you find him for me and make the request?"

"I will let you know in the morning," Grant said. "Now I have a request for you, Sam. Don't let me down. This project is far too important to fail."

"I won't, General. You have my word," Tillman said.

"Let's drink to that," Grant said and tossed back his bourbon.

After Breakfast, Tillman and Mary Elizabeth met Grant, Durant, and Casement in the lobby of the hotel. They took carriages to the railroad depot.

A hundred workers made up of Chinese, freed slaves, and Irish gathered around Durant's private car as he made a speech.

Mary Elizabeth checked out the private car assigned to her and Tillman. At forty feet long, it was larger than their cabin back home in the Big Woods. Besides its sheer size, it was lavish and ornate, equipped with expensive furniture, rugs, and two wood-stoves: one for cooking and one for heat.

Tillman and Grant met Tillman's crew of soldiers assigned to him at the car designated as the armory.

Grant gave Tillman the key.

Tillman opened the sliding door to the armory car.

"Sixty factory-new Henry rifles chambered in .44 rimfire," Grant said. "Each man draws one. The remaining forty stay in reserve for emergency use. There are also sixty factory-new Colt revolvers chambered in .45 Long Colt ammunition. Each man will draw one of those, as well. There is enough ammunition to invade Mexico, but more is always available upon request. Every man step up and draw your weapons."

After each man had drawn a rifle, revolver, and ammunition, Tillman, Grant, and Tillman's men listened to Casement speak to the hundred laborers surrounding Durant's private car.

A large mess tent was set up nearby. After Casement concluded his talk, everybody went in for lunch.

As expected, the men broke into groups. The freed slaves sat together, as did the Chinese and Irish.

After lunch, the work began. Reporters and photographers from around the country were on hand to document the event. Workers graded the land with plows and shovels, while others carried rails and ties and pounded the two together with sledgehammers and spikes.

Along the way, telegraph poles were added, following the tracks.

"Sam, take a ride with me," Casement said.

Tillman and Casement saddled their horses and rode west along the route Casement had mapped out after months of careful planning.

They dismounted, and Casement used his surveying equipment to determine the proper grading.

"We have a very long haul ahead of us, Sam," Casement said. "Through some very rough country and climate. Safety is my first concern. Safety for the men, for the project — for all of it."

Tillman lit his pipe and watched Casement work his instruments and make notations on his maps.

"Let's ride a few more miles," Casement said.

They rode another three miles and dismounted so Casement could survey the land and make more notations on his maps.

Casement lit a cigar and Tillman his pipe. They sat under a tree to smoke in the cool shade.

"When Grant told me he selected you to head up the security detail, I checked your military record and I was very impressed," Casement said. "I understand fully why he wanted you for the job."

"Thank you, General," Tillman said.

"It's John now, Sam," Casement said. "We'll be together for a long time to come, so let's do away with the formalities."

"All right, John," Tillman said.

"We have four months of good weather ahead of us, Sam," Casement said. "It's possible we can lay two hundred and fifty miles of track before we break for winter. Maybe even more, once the men gain some experience and we don't have too many bad weather days."

"Nebraska is new to me, General. I mean John. What can we expect in the way of Indians and such?" Tillman said.

"There is the Omaha Tribe west of here, the Pawnee near the North Platte River,

Arapaho, Cheyenne, and the Lakota north of the North Platte River," Casement said. "All but the Lakota and a small band of Pawnee have entered into peaceful treaties with the government."

"I expect we'll have some trouble out of somebody along the way," Tillman said.

Casement smiled. "I'd count on that, Sam," he said. "Let's head back before it gets dark on us."

Washington, 1901
Tillman finished his coffee and stood up from the table. He picked up his gear and started to walk to Roosevelt's home.

In the distance, he spotted the thick smoke of an approaching train.

He paused to check his watch. He walked to a busy street closer to the Capitol and decided to take a horse-drawn taxi the rest of the way to avoid being late.

The taxi reached Roosevelt's large home with two minutes to spare.

Roosevelt answered the door himself and ushered Tillman into the parlor, where his wife, Edith, waited with the six Roosevelt children. Of the six children, just Alice had been born to Roosevelt's first wife before she died in eighty-four.

Edith greeted Tillman with a warm hug,

and each Roosevelt child met Tillman with a handshake.

"Come on, Sam, let's see what we've got for supper," Roosevelt said.

On the street, the taxi with Brass as its passenger arrived at the Roosevelt home and paused.

"Do you wish to get out and for me to wait?" the driver said.

"Neither," Brass said. "I'd like you to take me to my hotel and then pick me up at six tomorrow morning. I will pay you very handsomely for your trouble."

"Very well, sir," the driver said.

CHAPTER TWENTY-ONE

1865

One way Mary Elizabeth found to occupy her time while Tillman was off riding with Casement or supervising his men was to bring water to the workers grooming the land and laying track.

One of the cars on the train carried nothing but water. Three times a day, Mary Elizabeth would fill a large bucket and carry it and a ladle to the men. Any man who wanted a drink could have one. Few refused.

At first some of the Irish workers refused to drink from the ladle a freed slave drank from, but they quickly learned it's better to have water than not, no matter what your skin color was.

Another way Mary Elizabeth found to occupy her time was to offer to mend the men's clothing free of charge. Once a week the men washed their clothing in boiling buckets of water, but few had the skill or the desire to mend, so most of them took her up on the offer to do their mending.

After a month, Mary Elizabeth was on a first-name basis with just about every man, Irish, freed slave, and Chinese.

All were most respectful to her, as not a man wanted to tangle with an angry Tillman if they weren't.

One afternoon, after lunch, Mary Elizabeth took tea at the table outside her riding car when a man she had never seen before rode up to her on horseback.

"Excuse me, ma'am, but I am looking for Sam Tillman," he said.

"He's a few miles down track," Mary Elizabeth said. "Is he expecting you?"

"My name is Glen Post, and he sent for me," Post said.

"He's spoken of you many times, Mr. Post," Mary Elizabeth said. "Come, have a cup of tea with me and wait for him."

Post dismounted, sat with Mary Elizabeth, and they chatted while they drank tea.

"You served with Sam in the war, didn't you?" Mary Elizabeth said as she filled Post's cup with tea.

"For about sixteen months or so, until he was recruited by General Grant to head up a special squad," Post said.

"Sam never speaks of the war," Mary Elizabeth said. "I only found out by accident, when General Grant called him a horse soldier, that he wasn't a regular soldier."

"I learned early on in the war that talking is not Sam's way," Post said. "He once told me bragging is a weakness he never wants to be accused of."

"That sounds like my husband," Mary Elizabeth said.

"When will he be back?" Post said.

"Around six tonight or so," Mary Elizabeth said. She saw the look on Post's face and chuckled. "But you can probably ride west for a few miles and catch him. He's with General Casement."

"General Casement?" Post said.

"He's the chief engineer for the railroad expansion project."

"I served under him after Sam left the cavalry to serve under Grant," Post said.

"If you ride west a few miles, you should meet up with them both," Mary Elizabeth said.

"Much obliged," Post said.

He mounted his horse and rode west into the countryside past the men laying track.

Post found Tillman, Casement, and three other men armed with Henry rifles in a field where Casement was surveying the land with his equipment.

"I'll be damned. You made it," Tillman said as he shook Post's hand.

"I wouldn't miss being a part of this," Post said.

"Glen, this is the chief engineer for the railroad, General John Casement," Tillman said.

"Hello, General. I served under you for nearly two years," Post said.

Casement looked at Post for a few seconds. "First Sergeant Post," he said. "I remember you clearly. Well, I'll also be damned."

Post and Casement shook hands.

"Good to have you aboard," Casement said.

While Casement returned to his equipment, Tillman and Post stood off to the side.

"I assume you met my wife," Tillman said.

"She told me where to find you, Post said.

"Did she offer you tea?"

Post grinned. "She did."

"God-awful stuff, but she likes it."

"Sam, I think we're done for today," Casement said.

"Mr. Durant, this is Glen Post, my assistant chief of police," Tillman said.

Durant and Casement were in Durant's private car, studying Casement's maps at a large table.

"Mr. Post, welcome aboard," Durant said.

"Thank you, Mr. Durant," Post said.

"Sam, I'd like to plan a three-day trip to survey the land up ahead," Casement said. "First thing in the morning."

"I'll get a crew together," Tillman said.

Seventy miles from Omaha, the workers lived in tents. Two men to a tent, each with a comfortable cot.

The mess tent was large enough to house one hundred men per meal. Another large tent with a wood floor and tables served as a saloon. Portable showers, with water supplied through barrels with mesh screens, and outhouses were also part of what was quickly becoming a traveling city.

As second in command, Post was allowed a tent to himself.

Workers were paid every two weeks. It was Tillman's duty to make sure each worker received his pay in cash. Every man had to sign for his money. If he couldn't write, he made his mark.

Tillman took a crew of four men with him when he and Casement left to survey the land. They planned on returning in six days.

Tillman left Post in charge of the security detail.

While Tillman was away, Mary Elizabeth requested to see Durant.

He received her in his private car.

"What may I do for you, Mrs. Tillman?" Durant said.

"A pastor," Mary Elizabeth said.

"What? Excuse me, did you say a pastor?" Durant said.

"There is a saloon, why not a pastor?" Mary Elizabeth said. "I'm sure many of the men would enjoy a Sunday service, wouldn't you agree?"

"To be honest, I hadn't thought about it," Durant said.

"Just because we're in the wilderness doesn't mean we should lack spirituality," Mary Elizabeth said.

"This is a working camp, Mrs. Tillman," Durant said. "And the men aren't exactly what I would call spiritual."

"Even a working man has a soul, Mr. Durant," Mary Elizabeth said.

Durant sighed. "I'll ask the men," he said. "But it's their decision, not mine. Agreed?"

"Agreed," Mary Elizabeth said.

Durant stepped into the mess tent when it was at capacity and asked to have the flaps closed.

He helped himself to a cup of coffee and

stood before the men.

"Men, we've only scratched the surface of this journey," Durant said. "It's a long road ahead of us. With that in mind, I've been asked the question, what do the men want? I've been told that it would be a good idea if we had a pastor for Sunday services. What say you men?"

At first, no one said a word, but then an Irish worker at a rear table stood up. "Mr. Durant, I think I speak for most men in this room when I say I'd rather have a whore to keep me warm at night than a pastor."

"I see," Durant said. "All right, by a show of hands who would like a pastor for Sunday services?"

About twenty men held up their hands.

"And who would rather a whore?" Durant said.

About eighty hands went up.

"I see. Thank you, gentlemen. I'll get back to you," Durant said.

"That was a good day's work, gentlemen," Casement said. "Twenty miles surveyed before dark."

"Coffee's hot and supper is cooking," Tillman said.

Tillman's four men sat around the campfire as Casement joined them.

"Any bumps in the road?" Tillman said as he handed Casement a cup of coffee.

"No, and I don't expect any for the next hundred miles," Casement said. "It's down the road we can expect more challenging terrain to deal with. Mountains, rivers, and harsh environments, for sure."

"Rivers I expect you can build bridges across, but how do you plan to deal with mountains?" Tillman said.

"If we can't go around them, we'll go through them," Casement said.

"Like it says in the good book," Tillman said.

By early October, the nights were chilly enough that the men used the small wood-stoves in their tents for heat.

The workers were skilled enough that they were averaging three miles of new track per day.

Any differences the Irish had with the freed slaves were mostly worked out, and many considered themselves friends with men of a different race.

The Chinese workers kept to themselves and went out of their way to bother nobody.

Durant called a meeting with Casement, his engineers, and Tillman.

In his private car, Durant asked the question, "Mr. Casement, how far can we go before winter shuts us down?"

"If we don't see a lot of snow, until January, when a deep frost sets in," Casement said. "The land will be too frozen to grade properly, even if we don't get snow."

"Mr. Tillman, how many men do you figure it will take to guard the supply trains and equipment?" Durant said.

"Ten should do," Tillman said.

By mid-November, they were two hundred and fifty miles west of Omaha. The workers had become very proficient at not only laying track, but at relocating what had become a traveling city.

Every twenty miles, the men would disassemble the tents and move them with skilled competence.

On a six-day scouting trip with Casement, Tillman and his four men spotted a hunting party of Omaha warriors. Tillman counted at least twenty of them. They stayed in the distance and watched as Casement surveyed the land.

"What do you think?" Casement said.

"I think they're sizing us up," Tillman said. "Trying to figure if twenty warriors with bows can take six men with Henry rifles."

"Can they?" Casement said.

"No, but that won't stop them from trying if they've got a mind to," Tillman said. "Go about your work, and I'll keep an eye on them."

Tillman got his binoculars and studied the Omaha warriors. They were handsome people for sure, and they rode bareback over a horse blanket.

A muscular warrior in front appeared to be leading the bunch. He sat on his horse without moving as he watched Tillman's group.

Then the lone warrior slowly moved his horse forward.

"General, you best quit what you're doing and get behind the men," Tillman said.

"Trouble?" Casement said.

"I'm not sure yet," Tillman said.

The lone warrior rode closer until he was about two hundred yards away, and then he stopped.

"Looks like he wants a parlay," Tillman said.

"You're not going out to see him?" Casement said.

"I always believe in being friendly to a man looking to talk," Tillman said.

"Sam?" Casement said.

"Don't worry, General. If they meant to

hit us, he wouldn't have come alone,"
Tillman said. "He's done the math and
knows six Henry rifles outweigh his twenty
warriors."

Tillman tied his neckerchief around the
front of his Henry rifle, mounted his horse,
and rode out to meet the lone warrior.

When ten feet separated Tillman from the
warrior, the warrior dismounted.

Tillman dismounted and the two met,
separated by less than a yard.

The warrior spoke in French.

Tillman shook his head. "English only,
I'm afraid," he said.

"My English not so good as my French,"
the warrior said.

Tillman nodded. "I am called Tillman.
How are you called?"

"In English I am called Spotted Hawk."

"It's my pleasure to know you, Spotted
Hawk," Tillman said.

"We are returning from a hunt and saw
you down there," Spotted Hawk said. "What
are you looking at?"

"The land for the railroad," Tillman said.

"The iron horse?"

"Yes."

"We saw the iron horse east of the town
called Omaha," Spotted Hawk said.

"The plan is to connect the entire country

with the iron horse," Tillman said. "From one side to the other."

"You will take much land to do this," Spotted Hawk said.

"Some, but not your land," Tillman said. "Just what is needed for the tracks for the iron horse to travel on."

"Some Cheyenne and most Lakota will fight you over the land," Spotted Hawk said.

"I hope not," Tillman said. "We want only peace. The railroad is a peaceful operation that will only help everybody, Cheyenne and Lakota alike."

"Do you have white man's medicine?" Spotted Hawk said.

"Yes, much."

"A doctor?"

"Yes."

"Bring your doctor to this spot in three days," Spotted Hawk said. "Our chief is very sick. He burns with fever."

Tillman nodded. "We'll be here," he said.

Tillman mounted his horse and returned to Casement.

"They won't bother you," he said. "I have to return to camp for medicine and Durant."

"Why?" Casement said.

"Their chief is sick."

■ ■ ■ ■

"Are you out of your mind, Mr. Tillman?" Durant said. "I'm not going anywhere."

"Right now those Nebraska Omaha are friendly, and I'd like to keep it that way," Tillman said. "Or would you rather incite a thousand Omaha warriors against me and my twenty men? Change your clothes, get your medicine bag, and I'll get us some fresh horses and supplies."

Durant frowned.

"In case you were wondering, Mr. Durant, that wasn't a request," Tillman said.

Tillman and Durant sat on their horses in the open field and waited.

Down below, Casement and Tillman's four men stood and watched.

"Well, where is he?" Durant said.

"There," Tillman said.

Spotted Hawk rode alone as he came over the hill to Tillman and Durant.

"Spotted Hawk, this is Doctor Thomas Durant," Tillman said.

"My chief burns," Spotted Hawk said. "I will take you to him."

The reservation of about one hundred and thirty thousand square acres was a half-day's ride from the field.

Tillman and Durant were surprised to find most of the two thousand Omaha Indians lived in cabins.

Tillman was also surprised to learn that Durant spoke fluid French and talked to Spotted Hawk and others in French while in the chief's cabin.

"He has pneumonia," Durant told Spotted Hawk after examining the chief. "He is old and weak, but I think I can pull him through."

After three days and nights of round-the-clock care, the old chief, while still very ill, was out of danger.

"I am leaving you this bottle of medicine and this bottle of pills and a spoon," Durant said. "Give him one pill three times a day and one spoon of the liquid medicine twice a day. Make sure no one besides the chief uses the spoon."

Spotted Hawk took the bottles and spoon.

Durant turned to Tillman. "When does Casement expect the tracks to reach that field?" he said.

"Ten days at most," Tillman said.

"I will return to check on the chief at that time," Durant said.

For Thanksgiving, Durant sent the first two

cars back to Omaha to pick up twenty-four turkeys for the workers.

The day was declared a holiday for the workers. They feasted on turkey with all the trimmings and pumpkin pie in the mess tent.

Tillman, Mary Elizabeth, Post, and all of Tillman's men joined in, along with Durant and Casement.

Although the Chinese workers had no idea what the celebration was about, they enjoyed themselves immensely.

Two days later, they reached the field where Tillman and Durant had met Spotted Hawk. Durant and Tillman rode to the reservation to check on the old chief.

To their surprise, the old chief was up and on his feet.

Durant gave him a thorough examination and, while the pneumonia was still present in his lungs, Durant was confidant the old chief would be around awhile longer. He gave another bottle of medicine and pills to Spotted Hawk and told him to continue the process until the old chief was back to full strength.

By mid-December, work slowed somewhat as the ground hardened by overnight frosts. Durant, Casement, and Tillman held a meeting in Durant's car to discuss the coming winter.

"We might be able to get another week out of the men before the frost settles in permanently," Casement said. "After that, work shuts down until mid- to late-March, depending on the snowfall."

"We'll break camp a week before Christmas and ride back to Omaha," Durant said. "Mr. Tillman, you and your men are tasked with guarding the cars loaded with material over the winter months. You will have two cars to sleep in. Food and supplies will be sent the first of each month until March. Make sure every man is paid in full before we break camp."

"When work resumes, we will explore the option of building our own towns along the way to wait out the winter," Casement said. "Those towns can be useful as supply depots as we continue west."

Afterward, Tillman discussed the situation with Mary Elizabeth.

"I don't see why I can't stay the winter with you," she argued. "The car is very comfortable, and we can be together."

"I need you to do something for our future, honey," Tillman said. "I've wired my father to meet you in Omaha. I have four thousand dollars and . . ."

"Four thousand?"

"Yes, four thousand," Tillman said. "Over the winter, I'd like you and my father to buy as much land in Montana as possible. Land that can be added on to as we go along. Right now Montana is a wilderness, but it won't be for much longer. We've got to get our land before the big ranchers discover it and gobble it all up."

"March is three months away," Mary Elizabeth said.

"That's nothing compared to four years," Tillman said.

"All right, Sam," Mary Elizabeth said. "I'll do it because it's our future, but I won't like being away from you again, especially for Christmas."

"I won't either, honey, but this is necessary for that future you just mentioned," Tillman said.

A week later only Tillman, Post, and nine of Tillman's men remained behind to protect the valuable cars of railroad property left behind.

1901
Washington, D.C.
Tillman and Roosevelt were having coffee on the front porch of Roosevelt's home. Roosevelt smoked a cigar, Tillman his pipe.

"It's a fine life you've built for you and

your family, Ted," Tillman said. "It seems like only yesterday you were a tenderfoot lost in the woods. Look at you now, vice-president of the United States."

"I'll tell you the truth, Sam. I hate the job," Roosevelt said. "Too slow and confining for my taste."

"Give yourself time. You'll get the hang of it," Tillman said. "You didn't start out to be a top-notch lawman or Rough Rider, did you?"

"Dammit Sam, why can't you stay another day?" Roosevelt said.

"I've got to finish this final assignment," Tillman said. "And then I'll see you at my retirement shindig."

Tillman and Roosevelt stood and shook hands. "Write me a good speech," Tillman said.

"You bet," Roosevelt said.

"And try not to lie about me too much," Tillman said.

"I can't promise that," Roosevelt said with a grin.

Roosevelt stayed on the porch until Tillman was out of sight, then he opened the door and went inside.

As Tillman walked to the livery stable to retrieve Blue, he spotted a horseless carriage parked in front of a private home.

The roof on the horseless carriage was down, and some kids were playing on the seats, while others were sitting on the front hood.

Tillman paused and looked at the kids.

"Does this carriage belong to you boys?" Tillman said.

A boy on the hood said, "Who wants to know?"

Tillman moved his jacket to expose his badge.

"I'm going to count to ten and then start arresting anybody who's still in my sight," Tillman said.

The boys scattered even before Tillman started to count. Tillman smiled and was about to continue walking, then paused to sniff the horseless carriage.

"By God, Jane was right. Stinks worse than a Kansas City outhouse in July," he said.

Tillman continued walking and didn't notice the taxi about a block behind him. Inside the taxi, Brass made a sketch of Tillman talking to the boys at the automobile.

When Tillman emerged from the ticket office, he walked to the hitching post where

Blue was tethered and rubbed the horse's neck.

"We got a few hours to kill before our train arrives," Tillman said. "I picked up a book in the ticket office."

Tillman walked to a bench, sat, took out his pipe, and lit a bowl.

He looked at the cover of the book and then put on his reading glasses.

Teddy Roosevelt and His Rough Riders.

"I'll be damned," Tillman said and opened the book to page one.

CHAPTER TWENTY-TWO

1901, Montana
Alice and Post took coffee on the front porch after supper so they could watch the sunset across the vast Montana sky.

"This is a beautiful place, Alice. And Sam's boys are fine men," Post said.

"It is beautiful, they are, and I am grateful to God neither sees fit to wear a badge," Alice said.

"I must say I agree with you on that last point, Alice," Post said.

"Don't get me wrong. The law is a necessary thing to keep order. Without it, there is no country. I just wish there was a way to do it without men getting killed," Alice said.

Post looked at the setting sun and sighed softly.

"I wish that very thing myself. Maybe someday it will be so," he said.

Alice looked at Post.

"We both know better than that," she said.

Post nodded his agreement.

"Alice, how did Sam come to acquire so much land in Montana so long ago?" he said. "He's never really talked about it."

"Thirty-five years ago, the government was practically giving the land away to anybody who wanted to raise cattle. Sam bought what he could when he could, and after ten years he had enough land to start building this house," Alice said.

"And his wife never got to live in it," Post said.

"No."

Alice and Post looked at the sky as it glowed orange and red.

"That would have broken most men, but not Sam. He was determined to have a place where his boys could grow up to become good men. After my husband died, I came to live here with Sam and helped raise the boys. Jake and Glen have done the lion's share of the work when Sam is off somewhere, like now," Alice said.

"Well, in a few weeks, Sam will be a full-time rancher and all this will be behind him," Post said.

Alice looked at Post with sadness in her eyes.

"Mr. Post, we both know somebody will be going home in a pine box," she said.

1866, Nebraska

January was bitter cold, and it snowed several times during the month. Tillman and his men spent most of the time inside the living cars with fires going in the wood-stoves.

Every hour, four men made patrols to check the equipment and supply cars.

Time was spent playing cards, reading from the extensive library provided by Durant, and playing chess and checkers.

One morning in mid-January, while Post and Tillman were making a patrol of the cars, Spotted Hawk and six of his warriors showed up on horseback. Dressed in heavy skins and furs to combat the cold, they looked more like bears on horseback than Omaha warriors.

"Spotted Hawk, what brings you out in such cold weather?" Tillman said.

Spotted Hawk and his men dismounted. "My warriors returned from a winter hunt and told me you and others stayed behind," Spotted Hawk said.

"To guard the railroad's property," Tillman said. "How is the old chief these days?"

"Well," Spotted Hawk said. "Even for a

man his age."

"Good," Tillman said. "You and your men come in out of the cold and share some lunch with us."

Spotted Hawk and his warriors had never seen anything like the interior of the railroad car. They seem amazed at the luxurious seats and furnishings. They were especially awed by the heavy curtains on the windows.

Tillman and Post served coffee to Spotted Hawk and his men.

"Find a comfortable seat," Tillman said.

Spotted Hawk and Tillman sat on the love seat and both men lit their pipes.

Post and another man fired up the cooking stove to prepare lunch.

"Good coffee," Spotted Hawk said.

"Why don't you take a couple of cans back with you?" Tillman said. "We've got more than we can drink, and we'll get a supply train the first of February."

"The old chief, he likes the . . . the sweet milk from the can," Spotted Hawk said.

"Condensed milk," Tillman said. "Take a few cans of that, too."

Lunch was beef stew with thick slices of bread. After lunch, Tillman and Spotted Hawk smoked their pipes with coffee. Tillman stuffed Spotted Owl's pipe with tobacco from his tin.

"Good smoke," Spotted Hawk said.

"I'll throw in a tin of tobacco with the coffee and milk," Tillman said.

Afterward, Tillman, Post, and the rest of the men watched Spotted Hawk and his warriors ride over the snow-covered hill.

"Fine people," Tillman said.

On the morning of January 31, Tillman, Post, and the men awoke to an attack from a band of Lakota warriors.

Post was returning from a trip to the outhouse when a Lakota arrow just missed his head and struck the side of the riding car.

Post ran into the car where Tillman and the others were already grabbing their Henry rifles.

"How many you figure there are?" Post said.

"Enough that they risked attacking us," Tillman said. "Casement said the Lakota refused to sign a treaty, so they're letting us know they're still around and have got a good grouch on."

"Think they'll try to burn us out?" one of the men said.

"Too much snow and ice on the cars," Tillman said. "My guess is they'll try to rush us and overpower us with numbers."

"What do you want to do, Sam?" Post said.

"Glen, you and Sergeant McCoy and Corporal McCray put on your warmest clothes, grab two blankets and a few boxes of ammunition for your Henry rifle, we're going up top," Tillman said. "The rest of you men open the windows and be prepared to shoot anything that moves."

Tillman and Post took the roof of one car, while McCoy and McCray took the other. They faced north to the hills. South was lowland, and the Lakota warriors would stick to the high ground.

After thirty minutes, Post said, "Sam, do you see anything?"

"No, but let's not take naps just yet," Tillman said.

At that moment, a dozen flaming arrows came flying over the over the hill and struck the sides of the railroad cars.

"Lieutenant?" McCoy shouted.

"Too much snow and ice to burn, so don't worry about it," Tillman said. "Worry about those warriors about to charge us."

Twenty Lakota warriors came charging over the hill armed with tomahawks and bows.

"They've probably never seen a Henry rifle," Tillman said. "Let's introduce them to each other."

Tillman, Post, McCoy, and McCray opened fire, as did the men inside the car. They cut down six of the warriors.

The remaining fourteen warriors took cover in the snow, and another dozen appeared directly behind them.

"They're going to rush us in waves," Tillman said. "Get ready, boys."

Flaming arrows struck the cars and a few hit the rooftops. Tillman grabbed an arrow, broke it in half, and tossed it to the ground.

"Ready yourselves, boys. Here they come," Tillman said.

Two dozen Lakota warriors ran down the snow-covered hill. Tillman and the others opened fire, dropping another five warriors.

The rest of the natives took cover in the snow, while another dozen came up behind them.

"Sam, another few rounds like that, and they'll be in our laps," Post said.

"I know it," Tillman said. "Everybody get down and form a firing line from the ground before they hit us again."

Tillman, Post, and the remaining nine men formed a crescent shape on the ground.

"Anything comes in your line of fire, shoot it," Tillman said. "And stay low on your belly. They have to stand up and expose themselves to get off a shot."

Thirty Lakota warriors stood and charged as arrows flew.

Another half dozen were cut down before they took cover in the snow. Yet another dozen came up behind them.

"Dammit, Sam, they're less than a hundred and fifty yards away now," Post said.

"Reload your Henrys to maximum capacity," Tillman said. "We got to take out as many as possible on the next charge."

They warriors charged again and eight were taken down, but twenty more came up behind them in the snow.

"They'll be on us for sure, the next charge," Tillman said. "Best ready yourselves, boys. We're in for a fight."

Tillman, Post, and the men quickly reloaded their Henry rifles and waited for the next onslaught.

More than fifty Lakota warriors stood and, as arrows fired, they charged with tomahawks.

"Hold fire until I give the order," Tillman shouted.

When the warriors were fifty yards away, Tillman shouted, "Fire at will."

The powerful Henry rifles cut down every Lakota warrior in their paths, but enough Lakota were about to get through the line when Spotted Hawk and fifty of his men rode into the pass from the west.

They charged the Lakota warriors and drove them back up the hill until they were out of sight.

"I'll be damned," Tillman said.

Tillman, Post, and Spotted Hawk took coffee inside Tillman's car, while Spotted Hawk's men allowed the Lakota warriors to gather up their dead.

"How did you happen by?" Tillman said.

"A hunting party saw the Lakota on the move," Spotted Hawk said. "We knew they would be coming here. They won't come back or risk war with my people."

"I am grateful to you, Spotted Hawk, and so are my people," Tillman said. "Is there anything you need?"

"Medicine. Some fresh meat, if you have," Spotted Hawk said.

"The supply train will be here in two days. Come back in three," Tillman said.

Once the Lakota warriors had cleaned up their dead, Tillman and Spotted Hawk shook hands outside the car, and Spotted Hawk and his warriors rode off.

"Glen, let's send a telegram to Omaha," Tillman said.

"I'll get the railroad telegraph box," Post said.

Durant and Casement made the trip on the supply train. They carried several letters from Mary Elizabeth, along with a large shipment of fresh supplies.

"It appears we owe Spotted Hawk and his people a great deal," Durant said after Tillman made a full report.

"It's likely none of us would be here if they hadn't showed up when they did," Tillman said.

"We should stay the night and greet them in the morning," Casement said.

"I agree," Durant said.

While supplies were unloaded, Tillman found a quiet spot and read the letters from Mary Elizabeth.

In the first letter she wrote that things were fine in the Big Woods, and she missed him and all that.

In the second letter she wrote that she and his father met with the land department in Washington and purchased several thousand acres of prime cattle country near a settlement along the Yellowstone River. The country was wide open and protected by army outposts along the river. A governor was appointed to oversee the newly formed

Montana Territory. Future land purchases would go through the just-formed capital city of Bannack.

"We're on our way," Tillman said as he tucked the letters into his pocket.

The following morning, Spotted Hawk and ten of his warriors arrived and were surprised to receive crates of blankets, coats, canned goods, and medicines. One crate contained one dozen Henry rifles, a gift from the railroad.

"Sam will teach you how to use the rifles, which will make hunting game much easier," Durant said.

"You bet," Tillman said.

"How is the old chief?" Durant said.

"He has regained his strength," Spotted Hawk said.

"Good. Tell him I wish him well," Durant said. "Can you remember my instructions about the use of medicine?"

"Yes."

"Glen and I will help bring the supplies to the reservation. There we will teach you how to shoot," Tillman said.

1901, Montana
Post and Alice took coffee on the porch after breakfast. The morning sun was warm, the vast sky clear and bright.

Both were surprised to see Glen and Jake ride Post's buggy to the porch with their horses in tow.

"It's been a week," Glen said. "We figured you might want to head over to Miles City and catch the train."

"I appreciate the gesture, boys," Post said. "But I gave your father my word I'd wait ten days. In forty years, I've never broken my word to him. I'm not starting now."

"I told Jake you'd say that, but he wouldn't listen," Glen said.

"Boys, I could use a little exercise," Post said. "How about we dig some postholes."

Chapter Twenty-Three

Nebraska, 1866

Work resumed in late March, and the men were averaging three and a half miles of new track per day.

Durant kept his word to Mary Elizabeth, and to the men as well.

Supplies were brought in to build a traveling church for those who wished to worship, and also to build a whorehouse for those who wished to partake. The church was front and center, the whorehouse behind the mess tent out of sight.

Eight women worked in the whorehouse. After work hours, the men lined up for a visit.

Casement, Tillman, and five of Tillman's men made long scouting expeditions for Casement's plans. By midsummer, they'd completed an additional two hundred and forty miles of track.

At the North Platte River, Casement drew

up plans for a bridge across the river, a distance of about two thousand feet.

Casement then took over the duty of construction manager while General Grenville Dodge was brought in to take over the duties as engineer.

At the North Platte River, construction of tracks stopped and every man, under the direction of Casement, participated in construction of the bridge.

Working sunup to sundown, the bridge took all summer and fall to complete. By December, the bridge was fully constructed.

Right after Christmas, construction was halted until the spring thaw.

Mary Elizabeth returned to the Big Woods with another four thousand dollars of investment money.

Dodge stayed behind and wanted to plan the continued route westward. Tillman was granted an additional ten men for security and, by the first of January on 1867, the camp was a ghost town.

Dodge planned to find a new route into Wyoming Territory that was quicker than the original route. He set out with Tillman, five men, and a month's worth of supplies.

Tillman put Post in charge of the men guarding the camp. On a frosty January morning, he, Dodge, and Tillman's five men set out to explore a new westward route.

Snow was light, despite frigid temperatures, and they were able to cover twenty miles a day, making frequent stops for Dodge to map out his plans.

Dodge took them along part of the South Platte River in western Nebraska and into Wyoming Territory. Dodge's new route, besides being a less gradual path, saved about a mile of track.

Tillman supplemented their supplies by hunting deer and wild turkeys along the way. In that way, they were able to stay out an extra two weeks.

When they returned to camp in mid-February, Dodge set about mapping his routes for the spring.

Tillman had several letters from Mary Elizabeth waiting for him. She and her father had purchased several thousand additional acres of land abutting the several thousand they already owned and, according to the Montana Territory governor, the number of acres for sale was in the millions.

Tillman's father planned a visit to Montana to access the land in the spring. Mary Elizabeth wanted to accompany him, so she wouldn't rejoin Tillman until sometime in mid-April.

The first of April, Durant, Casement, and

the entire workforce returned to the railroad camp to resume work.

Following Dodge's new route, the crew was able to lay three and a half miles or more of new track per day.

The camp, which was essentially a small town by this point, was moved every twenty miles.

Mary Elizabeth arrived on May first, with the supply train.

"Oh, Sam, you should see Montana," she said when they had dinner in their private car. "As wide open as the sky, and fields so green, they made me dizzy. Our land is just a speck on the open range."

"We need more land to start our ranch. A lot more land," Tillman said.

"Yes, but we are off to a very good start," Mary Elizabeth said.

"I have to make the most of this job while I can, honey," Tillman said. "When the railroad connects, the job ends, and so does this high money."

"In two years we'll have . . ."

"Not nearly enough," Tillman said. "But, like you said, it's a good start."

"Sam, what about a family?" Mary Elizabeth said.

"We can think about family when this job is over," Tillman said. "A railroad car is no place to have a baby."

By June, they'd moved the town several more times and it grew even larger, in part due to business from back east setting up shops with permission from Durant.

A blacksmith shop, butcher shop, and clothing store were added to the list of businesses included in the portable railroad town.

In July, several dozen workers were added to the force. Track production averaged four miles a day.

Some of the new workers weren't exactly savory. In August, in the large tent that served as the saloon, a man named John Savoy, in a drunken fit of rage, shot and killed a Chinese worker he believed cheated him at cards.

Tillman, already asleep in bed, was immediately sent for. He entered the saloon dressed in his pants and nightshirt and wearing his Colt revolver.

Savoy was at the bar with a glass of whiskey. His Remington revolver rested on the bar near his right hand.

"What's happened here?" Tillman said.

"This man here shot the Chinaman," the bartender said.

"Damn right, I did," Savoy said. "Cheated at cards. I'd shoot him again."

By this time, Post and several other rail-road police armed with rifles had entered the saloon.

"He didn't cheat, and he wasn't armed," the bartender said.

"Mister, turn around," Tillman said. "You're under arrest."

"The hell you say," Savoy said.

"Mister, leave the gun on the bar, turn around, and put your hands up," Tillman said. "I won't ask again."

"Screw you, law dog," Savoy said as his hand inched to the revolver on the bar.

"Touch that gun, and I will kill you," Tillman said. "I promise you that."

Savoy grabbed his Remington, cocked it, but before he could fire, Tillman drew his Colt and shot him dead on the spot.

The shot echoed loudly inside the tent. Nobody moved or said a word as the echo faded.

"Goddammit," Tillman said.

"Jesus, Sam," Post said quietly.

Durant, Dodge, and Casement entered the tent.

"What happened here?" Durant demanded.

Mary Elizabeth rushed into the tent in time to witness Tillman slowly return his Colt to the holster.

"Sam," she cried.

Tillman put his arm around Mary Elizabeth's shoulder, then turned and exited the tent.

The following morning, when Tillman entered the mess tent at breakfast, every man fell silent.

Tillman stood in the center of the tent.

"From today, if any man has a beef with another man, it is to be settled with fists," Tillman said. "In a square, and which I will referee. At the end of the fight, both men will shake hands, and that will be the end of it. Any man who raises a gun to another man while employed by the railroad, I will personally hang. I guarantee you that."

Construction moved forward without incident. By fall, they were close to Wyoming Territory.

Dodge, Tillman, and a few of Tillman's men scouted ahead. Dodge selected an area in Wyoming Territory where they would pause for the winter.

In December they reached the area Dodge selected.

"This area will become the hub for the railroad," Dodge told Durant and Casement in a meeting. "Rather than send the men home, I suggest we build a permanent settlement here that the railroad can use as a crossroads, not just east and west, but north and south."

Durant sent a telegraph to the stockholders in New York for funds to construct the town. In December, construction was underway.

Casement's ability to plan construction proved invaluable. Within weeks, a town had begun to take shape.

Mary Elizabeth returned to the Big Woods on the supply train the first of January, 1867.

As the town took shape as a permanent settlement, Dodge and Tillman scouted ahead for railroad routes.

Dodge made plans to bridge Dale Creek, and designed a bridge.

By March, the town was complete. Durant named it Cheyenne, after the native tribes living in the territory.

Work resumed in April and, by June, construction was underway for the Dale Creek Pass.

Mary Elizabeth returned in May, after another trip to Montana with Tillman's father. Alice accompanied them. The news was that Alice would soon marry.

Cheyenne grew quickly as word spread about the new railroad town that would serve as a hub of transportation.

For months, Tillman and several of his men stayed behind to keep law and order in the new town until finally a sheriff was duly elected.

By September, the Dale Creek Bridge was complete and work laying track recommenced.

In October, Mary Elizabeth told Tillman she was pregnant.

"Pack your bags. You're going home on the next supply train," Tillman said.

"Honestly, Sam, I'm fine," Mary Elizabeth said.

"Maybe so, but this is no place for a pregnant woman, especially my wife," Tillman said. "I'll wire my father to pick you up in Omaha."

Reluctantly, Mary Elizabeth agreed.

In December, work stopped. Another town was built over the course of the winter. That town was named Laramie.

In January of 1868, two unexpected events took place.

An official letter from the United States Marshals Office arrived on the supply train addressed to Post.

After the war, Post applied for a position with the marshals, and his appointment as a deputy marshal was approved. He was to report to New Mexico Territory and assume his duties.

"I'm sad to see you go, Glen, but I understand," Tillman said.

"Sam, I'll stay if you ask," Post said. "I can request a delay in my appointment."

"No call for that," Tillman said. "The railroad job will be over in another year, and the marshal's job is permanent."

"Sam, you'd make a fine marshal," Post said.

"It's something to think about when this job has concluded," Tillman said.

Afterward, when he had some time alone, Tillman sat quietly in his car and read his mail.

Two letters from Mary Elizabeth, and one from his father.

It was the first letter his father had written, and Tillman opened it first. The news was bad.

Mary Elizabeth had suffered a miscarriage.

Chapter Twenty-Four

1901

Tillman ate dinner in the dining car and continued to read the dime novel about Roosevelt and his Rough Riders.

The novel covered Roosevelt's early life to his time as a deputy sheriff, and ended with his famous charge up San Juan Hill in Cuba.

Tillman read the chapter where a young Deputy Roosevelt single-handedly tracked down the bandits who stole his riverboat and brought them all to justice.

Tillman laughed so hard, he nearly spat his coffee onto the table.

"Oh, Ted," he said aloud, and removed his reading glasses.

At the end of the dining car, Brass made another sketch in his book. When he noticed Tillman about to stand, Brass got up quickly and left the car.

■ ■ ■ ■

1868

"What in God's name are you doing here, Sam?" Mary Elizabeth said when Tillman entered his parents' home.

"I've come to see about my wife," Tillman said.

Mary Elizabeth hugged him tightly. "I'm fine, Sam," she said.

"Where are my parents?" Tillman said.

"They went to town for supplies."

"I'd best get my horse into the barn before he freezes to death."

"I'll put on a pot of coffee."

After Tillman took care of his horse, he and Mary Elizabeth sat at the table with cups of coffee.

"The doctor said I'm fine and can have as many children as we want," Mary Elizabeth said. "He doesn't know why I had the miscarriage. He said it happens sometimes."

"What was it?" Tillman said.

"A girl."

"By God," Tillman said.

"We'll have more, Sam. Don't you worry," Mary Elizabeth said. "I'm at full strength, and next month, your father and I are returning to Montana to buy more land."

"You take it easy," Tillman said.

Mary Elizabeth grinned. "Me taking it easy won't get you any children," she said.

Work resumed in late March, and the crew worked its way toward Utah.

The terrain grew rockier and more dangerous. Dodge searched for ways around it. Even so, the crew averaged better than four miles of new track per day.

Mary Elizabeth returned on a supply train in May.

She glowed with health, a sight that greatly relieved Tillman.

During the summer Durant, Dodge, and Tillman met with a large group of Mormons in Utah Territory to recruit Mormon workers to help with blasting the way through the rugged Weber River Canyon.

Of the four tunnels blasted using the newly discovered nitroglycerin, the longest was seven hundred and fifty-seven feet long. Several fatal accidents occurred during the blasting process.

In December, the ground froze, the snow fell, and work stopped until spring. A town was constructed for the work crew to wait out the winter.

Mary Elizabeth once again went home to the Big Woods. In the spring, she and

Tillman's father would travel to Montana to buy more land.

1869

Spring came early, and work resumed in March.

Tillman and Dodge rode ahead. Dodge estimated that the Union Pacific and Central Pacific Railroads would join in May at Promontory Summit in Utah.

Durant desperately wanted to beat the Central Pacific Railroad to the summit. He promised each man a month's extra wages if they arrived first.

The meeting place for the two railroads was marked by a red flag.

Casement reported to Durant that the Central Pacific was on pace to reach the flag ahead of them.

"How is that possible?" Durant said.

"They have just five miles of track to lay tomorrow, while we have ten," Dodge said.

"What if we started at three in the morning, worked by torches, and my twenty men joined the crew? Could it be done?" Tillman said.

Dodge nodded. "It's worth a shot," he said.

On the morning of May 10, the entire crew, plus Tillman and his twenty men, started work just before three a.m.

Even Dodge and Casement joined in.

Mary Elizabeth, and even the prostitutes, helped out by bringing coffee, food, and water to the crew. The men worked without a break, and not a one of them complained.

By sunup, they's set down three miles of new track.

"Every man works," Tillman shouted to his men. "We got seven miles to go, men. So put your mind to it that we're going to get this done."

They ate as they worked. As they passed the five-mile mark, the men worked as if possessed.

"Two months' bonus if we beat the Central to the flag," Durant promised.

Fueled on by the desire to beat the Central Pacific to the flag — or by the promise of bonus money — the crew worked nonstop all afternoon.

Reporters and photographers from across the country had gathered to witness the connection of the two railroads.

The excitement built, as if the gathered crowd was witnessing a thoroughbred horse race.

The race to the flag was close, but the Union Pacific crew won the race by a mere few yards.

Photographers took dozens of photos. When Durant took the honor of driving in the final spike, known as the Golden Spike, reporters and photographers, as well as the entire crew, went wild.

In the crowd was John Campbell, the newly appointed Governor of Wyoming Territory.

At the ceremony that evening, Campbell approached Tillman.

"Mrs. Tillman, may I borrow your husband for a few minutes?" Campbell said.

"Certainly, sir," Mary Elizabeth said.

Tillman followed Campbell outside the tent to a quiet spot beside a railroad car. Campbell produced a silver flask, took a sip, and passed it to Tillman.

"I have been appointed by President Grant to serve as the first governor of Wyoming Territory," Campbell said. "My capital will be Cheyenne. Since its founding two years ago, it has grown into a hub for the railroad. It's an important town to Grant and to the railroad, Mr. Tillman. Very important."

Tillman took a sip from the flask and passed it back to Campbell.

"I know all that, Mr. Campbell. I helped build it and all the other towns along the way," Tillman said.

"I know, and I've spoken to Durant, Dodge, and Casement. All of them agree that you are my man to keep law and order in Cheyenne," Campbell said. "Right now it's a lawless place and needs law and order for it to thrive. As chief of railroad police, you are the perfect man for the job."

"A town needs a sheriff, not a . . ." Tillman said.

"Cheyenne is railroad property," Campbell said. "Federally owned. Your position as chief of railroad police is a federal appointment. A perfect marriage, so to speak."

"I pick my own deputies," Tillman said.

"Of course. You also get a house and five hundred dollars a month," Campbell said.

"Make it seven-fifty," Tillman said.

"That's agreeable," Campbell said.

"Allow me to talk to my wife," Tillman said.

"I'd expect you to. It's a big decision," Campbell said.

1901

Tillman returned to the dining car at seven in the evening for supper. He had read most of the dime novel by then and planned to finish the final few chapters over a steak.

He ordered coffee first and lit his pipe, put on his reading glasses, and opened the dime novel to read. A young, well-dressed woman in her twenties approached the table.

"Excuse me, sir, but may I share your table?" she said. "I'm traveling alone, and I could use some dinner-table conversation."

Tillman stood up and pulled the chair out for her, then returned to his seat.

"Sam Tillman, Tillman said.

"Victoria Dobbs of Philadelphia. I see by your badge that you are a US Marshal."

"For another few weeks," Tillman said.

"Retiring?"

"In another few weeks," Tillman said. "And you're the second young woman I've encountered inside a week who was traveling alone."

"I'm visiting Chicago, sir. You see, my father is in steel. We are quite well off, and I visit places like Chicago for the adventure," Victoria said.

"Adventure? In Chicago?"

"The museums, the theatre, the fine restaurants. Chicago has all of that and much more," Victoria said.

"And you consider that adventure? Eating in a restaurant?"

Victoria smiled sweetly. "I must sound silly to a man like you, don't I?" she said.

"Not at all. I'm just interested in what

young people think of the world these days," Tillman said.

"Seriously?"

"Yes."

"Why, the world is a fine place filled with new and exciting things. After I graduated the university, I had the desire to travel and see them for myself," Victoria said.

"And?"

"Honestly?"

"Yes."

"Sometimes I am so bored, I could just cry," Victoria said.

Tillman stared at Victoria with such a straight face that she broke out laughing.

The waiter arrived at the table. "What would you care for, miss?"

"Whatever the marshal is having," Victoria said.

The waiter nodded and went to the kitchen.

"Now, Marshal, you look like a man who has had quite a few adventures in his life. Please tell me about some of them," Victoria said.

After dinner, Tillman and Victoria ordered coffee and lingered at the table for a while.

"Have I offended you with some of my stories, Miss Dobbs?" Tillman said.

"On, no, sir. Quite the contrary. You have

stirred my blood, as if I were a child reading a dime adventure novel."

"But?"

"But I will never know such adventure or experience the dangers you have experienced. Mine is a life of soft pillows, fine food, and boring museums."

"I thought you were going to Chicago for the museums," Tillman said.

Victoria sighed. "I might as well be visiting a graveyard."

"I'll tell you what, young lady. You have a standing invitation to visit me at my ranch in Montana any time you wish. Call it a completion of your education. Of course, you'll have to work for your bed and breakfast," Tillman said.

"I would like that, Marshal. I would like that very much," Victoria said.

"My friends call me Sam," Tillman said.

"All right, Sam," Victoria said. "I'm afraid I must get some sleep. Would you escort me to my car?"

"My pleasure," Tillman said.

As Tillman took Victoria's arm and escorted her out of the dining car, Brass entered from the other door and discreetly followed them.

At Victoria's car, Tillman said, "Good night, Victoria. I hope you take me up on my offer."

"Marshal, perhaps we can breakfast together in the morning before we reach Chicago?" Victoria said.

"You bet. Have a good sleep, Victoria," Tillman said.

Tillman went to his sleeping car and sat on the bed. He removed the flask from his luggage and took a small sip. He opened his pocket watch and looked at the tiny picture of Mary Elizabeth on the inside cover plate.

"Victoria is a fine young woman, Mary Elizabeth," he said and took another sip. "There is hope for this generation yet."

CHAPTER TWENTY-FIVE

Cheyenne, 1870

With deputies McCoy, McCray, and two others from his squad of twenty, Tillman kept the peace in Cheyenne.

As the largest railroad town constructed along the route to Promontory Point, it was an important hub for the railroad. Supply trains regularly hooked up with routes north and south, and the growing repair yard and nearby army fort only served to increase the importance of the town.

Campbell was correct in that the new town was a wild and lawless place, not safe for women and children.

Tillman and his deputies worked quickly to institute law and order and establish the peace. Those quick with a gun found themselves arrested or dead. Horse theft or the rape of a woman likely drew a noose in Campbell's court as governor.

Tillman and Mary Elizabeth occupied a

fine house on the edge of town. From there she made two trips back to the Big Woods and then traveled to Montana with Tillman's father to buy land.

In early spring, Glen Post arrived in town with news.

Over dinner at their home, Post told Tillman and Mary Elizabeth that he had discussed the position of marshal of Colorado Territory with those in Washington and Tillman was selected for the position.

The position included a central office in Denver, with sixteen deputies to cover the entire territory, a salary of eight hundred a month, and a furnished home to start.

Mary Elizabeth had news of her own. She was three months pregnant.

"Colorado is wide open country," Tillman said. "It might be just the place to have our first child, away from all this railroad smoke and dirt."

"When does Sam have to report to Denver?" Mary Elizabeth asked Post.

"Thirty days."

"We have time to go to Montana and see about more land," Tillman said.

Tillman rented a buggy, and he and Mary Elizabeth road to their land in Montana. Tillman was astonished at the beauty of the territory.

"At last count, we have twelve thousand acres," Mary Elizabeth said.

"That sounds like a lot, but it's not nearly enough to support a herd of any size," Tillman said. "We'll need thirty thousand acres at minimum."

"That will take another four years," Mary Elizabeth said. "We could borrow the money from a bank."

"And have a bank own our land," Tillman said. "A ranch or a farm will lose money the first five years. I learned that from my parents and yours. If we can't meet the terms of the loan, the bank will foreclose on us, and there goes everything we worked for — up in smoke, including all the money we put into it."

"Four more years is a long time, Sam," Mary Elizabeth said.

"Which we will use to plan the building of our house," Tillman said. "And give our children a fine place to grow up in."

Denver, Colorado, 1870
Denver was a sprawling town of about four thousand residents. It was also home to the Denver Pacific Railroad that connected directly to Cheyenne in Wyoming.

With the Rocky Mountains to the west

and the high plains to the east, Denver was a sight to behold.

It was also home to Territorial Governor Edward McCook, who had also been appointed by President Grant.

Denver attracted the very rich, who saw the potential of Colorado, and also the very poor: outlaws and criminals who preyed on the wealthy.

Because it was a large territory to cover with just sixteen deputy marshals, Tillman quickly established that violators of the law would not be tolerated.

With fierce determination, Tillman and his deputies set out to rid the entire territory of outlaws and criminals.

Glen was born just before Thanksgiving. Tillman's parents came to visit for a month. After that, Mary Elizabeth's parents visited for another month.

By the spring of seventy-one, Mary Elizabeth was pregnant with their second child, whom they would name John, for Mary Elizabeth's father.

Post came for a visit in the summer and spent a week. Tillman had attracted the attention of the director of the service in Washington, and Post had been sent to see if Tillman would be interested in a supervisory position in the marshal's service in the

Capitol.

"A desk job," Tillman said.

"Most supervisory jobs are," Post said.

"Is that what you do these days, ride a desk?" Tillman said.

"I paid my dues," Post said. "And so did you, Sam, ten times over. Why not let someone else take the risks and dodge the bullets for a change?"

"We've got fifteen thousand acres of land in Montana," Tillman said. "In a few years, we'll be building a home and a ranch for our future and the future of our children. I can't do any of that sitting on my ass in Washington, getting fat and damn lazy."

"Sam, Glen can hear you. Watch your language," Mary Elizabeth said.

"Glen ain't but ten months old," Tillman said. "And my answer is no, I do not want to sit at a desk in Washington and grow fat and lazy. As soon as we have enough acres for our ranch, Mary Elizabeth and I are headed north to Montana, and there we will stay."

"I told them you'd say that," Post said. "And to be honest, Sam, I'm glad to hear it."

In early seventy-two, Jake was born. Tillman had close to eighteen thousand acres, and he and Mary Elizabeth were making plans to design a ranch house.

Colorado, 1874
In early fall, a gang of outlaws called the Beck brothers, who were wanted in four states, traveled to Colorado and hid out in a small township called Pueblo.

Besides the brothers, Slim Beck and Tony, the gang consisted of four other ruthless killers.

The Beck brothers cut a path across Texas, Oklahoma, Arkansas, and Kansas and finally burst into Colorado. Along the way, they robbed stagecoaches, banks, stole horses and cattle, murdered a dozen people, and raped the like number of women.

They stopped at nothing to get what they wanted.

Tillman took the railroad south to Colorado Springs and met four of his deputies. From there they rode south to Pueblo.

Pueblo was a town of only a few hundred people, but the Beck brothers had women friends who took them in and gave them sanctuary. The few hundred townspeople in the small community were too terrorized to do anything about the outlaws.

Except for a young Mexican boy. He sneaked away, reached the local county sheriff's office, and informed on the vicious gang. They had raped his mother, and the boy risked his life to reach the county sheriff.

It was the county sheriff who wired Tillman. On a beautiful spring morning, Tillman and his men met up with the county sheriff and his deputies, and they rode into Pueblo.

The Beck brothers and their gang were ready for them. A shootout in the town square lasted for an hour or more.

Four sheriff's deputies were wounded, as was one of Tillman's marshals, but the four members of the Beck brothers' gang were killed.

The Beck brothers hid behind the large fountain in the town square where they could have held out for hours.

Tillman gave them a chance to surrender. The Beck brothers answered with a barrage of bullets.

"That's enough," Tillman said. "By God, that's enough."

He mounted his horse and charged the fountain, taking the Beck brothers completely by surprise when he jumped the fountain and shot the both of them dead, but not before taking a bullet in the left leg.

While he was recovering from his wound,

Tillman received another visit from Glen Post.

"This comes from the top, Sam, from Grant himself," Post said. "He's appointing a young judge to Fort Smith in Arkansas and wants you to take charge of the territory until things calm down."

"Fort Smith," Tillman said.

"I know, Sam, I know," Post said. "But it's too important a town to fail, and Grant said he would sweeten the pot by adding bonus money to your pay."

"I'll need a few weeks to let my leg finish healing," Tillman said.

"That's fine, Sam. That's just fine," Post said.

Denver, 1879
Mary Elizabeth returned from Montana with Glen and Jake after checking on their land and house.

Tillman's father escorted them, and afterward they visited family in the Big Woods.

"Another six months, and the house will be ready," Mary Elizabeth reported. "Then the barn and corral, and in a year, we will be able to move in."

"How many acres will we have in another year?" Tillman said.

"Thirty thousand," Mary Elizabeth said.

"And not only that, the town of Miles City is growing into a fine town, and it's only thirty miles away."

"We're finally on our way, honey," Tillman said. "A real home and a ranch where our boys can grow to men and maybe we can see about a girl or two."

That night, as they ate dinner, Tillman noticed Mary Elizabeth's slight cough. She said she'd caught a chill from the Montana air, and that it was nothing.

However, the cough worsened. They ultimately went to see the doctor in Denver.

"Mrs. Tillman, I'd like you to see a doctor in Boston," the doctor said. "He's the best in the business at treating tuberculosis."

"Tuberculosis?" Tillman said. "It's just a cough, for God's sake."

"Marshal, your wife needs to see the doctor in Boston," the doctor said. "And the quicker, the better."

Tillman's parents stayed with Glen and Jake while Sam and Mary Elizabeth went to Boston.

"Mrs. Tillman, if you continue to live in Colorado, you will be dead within a year," the doctor in Boston said.

"We just built a house in Montana," Mary Elizabeth said.

"Montana will kill you even quicker, I'm

afraid," the doctor said. "If I sound blunt, it's because time is a factor here. You need a dry, arid climate, Mrs. Tillman, and the sooner, the better."

"Such as?" Tillman said.

"New Mexico or Arizona," the doctor said. "Arizona would be my first choice."

Tillman made the trip to Washington to request a transfer to Arizona Territory in person. The request was granted immediately.

Nineteen months later, Mary Elizabeth passed away.

Tillman held her hand as she took her final shallow breath.

Chapter Twenty-Six

1901

Tillman and Victoria had coffee after breakfast in the dining car. The train started to slow its speed as it approached the station in Chicago.

"I don't know why, Sam, but I suddenly feel very frightened," Victoria said.

"That's the anticipation of a new adventure still unwritten. Come, I'll walk you out," Tillman said.

With arms linked, Tillman and Victoria stood on the crowded platform.

"I don't know what to say, Sam," Victoria said.

"Say goodbye, and don't wait too long to come for a visit. I'm not getting any younger you know," Tillman said.

Tillman extended his right hand. Victoria looked at it.

"Oh, hell," Victoria said and reached up

to kiss Tillman on the cheek.

Then, with mist in her eyes, Victoria turned and walked to the end of the platform.

Tillman touched his cheek. "Well, how about that," he said.

He took out his pipe, lit it, and looked at the Chicago skyline in the distance. He stopped a passing conductor.

"How long is this layover?" Tillman said.

"About an hour."

"Obliged," Tillman said.

He walked to the end of the platform and entered the boxcar where Blue was the only horse on board.

Blue turned and showed excitement at seeing Tillman.

"I brought you a little something," Tillman said.

Tillman removed a handful of sugar cubes from a pocket and fed them to Blue.

"Stole them from the dining car. I expect you'll be cooped up in here another twenty-four hours or so. If we have a stop with a layover, I'll take you out for a run," Tillman said.

He fed Blue a few more cubes and rubbed his neck.

"I best get back before they leave without

me. Then where would you be?" Tillman said.

Walking back to his car, Tillman stopped the conductor.

"Do we have any long layover stops on the way to Laramie?" Tillman said.

"We do have one two-hour layover in Columbus, Nebraska, at six tomorrow morning," the conductor said.

"Obliged," Tillman said.

Before sunrise in Columbus, Nebraska, Tillman walked Blue to the edge of the deserted railroad platform.

The sky lightened a bit, and Blue started to fidget with anticipation.

"Easy, boy. We're almost there," Tillman said.

Slowly, the sky lightened and the ground began to glow. Tillman rubbed Blue's neck to steady the massive horse.

"Every sunrise is the same, and every sunrise is different, and I love every damn one of them," Tillman said aloud.

Tillman mounted the saddle and, with a tug of the reins, Blue jumped off the platform and they headed south.

From the shadows on the platform, Brass stepped forward and watched Tillman ride away.

■ ■ ■ ■

Tillman raced Blue until they were miles from the station. Blue's long, powerful legs ate up the ground until Tillman slowed the powerful horse to a trot and finally to a stop.

They faced the new sunrise and allowed themselves to be bathed in the light.

"Horseless carriage, my ass," Tillman said as he patted Blue's neck.

On the platform, Brass sat with his notebook and waited.

Brass stood when he spotted Tillman returning in the distance.

Tillman rode Blue at a moderate pace until they were a hundred yards from the station. Then Tillman tugged back on the reins to raise Blue's head, and Blue appeared to prance the last hundred feet to the station.

Brass watched in amazement.

In the boxcar, Tillman gave Blue a good brushing and then fed him a few more sugar cubes.

"Now you just sit tight until this afternoon, while I go have a talk with a nosy gossip," Tillman said.

■ ■ ■ ■

Brass sat in a seat beside the window and sketched in his notebook with a charcoal pencil.

The likeness was of Tillman and his prancing horse.

Brass didn't notice Tillman until Tillman was in the seat opposite him.

"Now then, suppose you tell me why you've been following me since Omaha and before," Tillman said.

For a moment, the startled Brass was taken aback.

"I'm . . . I'm a reporter," Brass said.

"I know who you are. We met a week ago, remember? What do you want?" Tillman said.

"A story," Brass said.

"A story? A story about what?" Tillman said.

"Why, about you," Brass said.

"Me? What are you talking about?" Tillman said.

"I'm talking about Sam Tillman, one of the most famous marshals there is, visiting Wyatt Earp, Bat Masterson, and Vice President Roosevelt. I even heard you went to see Calamity Jane, but I haven't confirmed that yet," Brass said.

"What of it?" Tillman said.

"My job is to report the news, Marshal," Brass said.

"How is a man visiting some old friends a news story?" Tillman said.

"Because I don't think that's what it is," Brass said.

"You don't, huh?" Tillman said.

"No, I don't. It is my opinion that you are a news story, and it is my job to uncover what that story is," Brass said.

"Does that include spying on people?" Tillman said. "Sneaking around behind their backs?"

"The First Amendment guarantees the right to a free press inside the public sector or square, Marshal," Brass said.

"Does it guarantee you won't get a cracked skull in the process?" Tillman said.

Brass looked at Tillman as Tillman stood up.

"Do you carry a firearm?" Tillman said.

"No, of course not."

"Maybe you should get acquainted with the Second Amendment as well. Where I'm headed, you just might need one," Tillman said. He looked at Brass's sketch. "And that doesn't look a thing like me, or my horse either, for that matter."

Tillman opened the sliding door and exited the car.

Brass inhaled deeply, then wiped a bead of sweat from his forehead.

In the dining car, after breakfast, Tillman lingered over a cup of coffee and his pipe. He put on his reading glasses, opened the dime novel about Roosevelt, and read the final chapter.

"Let's see what old Teddy has in store for me this morning," he said.

CHAPTER TWENTY-SEVEN

South Dakota, 1886

In late March, Tillman, stationed in Montana at this time, set out after a group of nine dangerous outlaws wanted on federal warrants.

The gang was spotted along the Little Missouri River in North Dakota. Tillman wired a deputy marshal named Seth Bullock in the town of Deadwood. They had crossed paths before, going back to the murder of Bill Hickok. Tillman took the railroad out of Miles City directly to Deadwood in South Dakota.

Tillman met Bullock in the Nuttal and Mann's Saloon, where Wild Bill Hickok had been murdered a decade earlier. The saloon had burned down once and had since been rebuilt.

Over coffee, Tillman and Bullock made plans to pursue the outlaw gang.

"They were last seen along the Little Missouri near a town called Medora," Tillman said. "We best rent a mule and pick up a hundred pounds of supplies. This could take a while."

"Stay at the hotel tonight as my guest, Marshal," Bullock said. "I'm part owner of the hotel. We'll leave at first light. We can take the railroad north to Medora and start tracking them from there."

Spring in Deadwood, South Dakota, was close to winter in Medora, North Dakota. Founded along the railroad lines just a few years earlier, Medora boasted a mere several hundred residents, a town square, and not much else to brag about.

With the mule loaded with supplies in tow, Tillman and Bullock rode west along the Little Missouri River, hoping to pick up the outlaws' trail.

Parts of the Little Missouri were still frozen, and large sections of ice floated freely on the parts that were open water.

Tillman and Bullock were experienced outdoorsmen. Among their gear was a tent large enough to sleep four. They also brought extra bedrolls and blankets for the horses and mule.

Tillman and Bullock sat in front of a warm fire and ate a hot supper of beef stew with bread and coffee sweetened with a little condensed milk.

"We rode all day and didn't see so much as a snapped twig," Bullock said. "Maybe we're on the wrong path?"

"Maybe, but we need to be sure," Tillman said. "We'll give it another day or so before we turn around. Nine outlaws just don't disappear into thin air."

After eating, Tillman filled two cups with hot coffee.

"Want me to sweeten that?" Bullock said. "I've got a flask of Kentucky bourbon."

"I'll take an ounce," Tillman said.

After Bullock added bourbon to the coffee, he rolled a cigarette and Tillman lit his pipe.

"How are your boys, Sam?" Bullock said.

"Just fine," Tillman said. "My sister is at the ranch full-time now. They're a handful, but she rules the roast. They're growing up good boys, mindful, like their mother."

"Glad to hear it, Sam," Bullock said.

"What about yours?" Tillman said.

"Oh, Martha is fine, and the kids are well enough," Bullock said. "Now that I own a hotel and half of the Nuttal and Mann's Saloon, she's after me to give up the badge."

"But?"

Bullock grinned. "But for the same reason

you still wear yours. It's the only thing I'm really good at."

Tillman nodded. "Tomorrow we'll do twenty miles. If we don't pick up any signs, we'll backtrack. But right now I'm going to do the other thing I'm really good at."

"What's that?" Bullock said.

"Sleep."

"Hell, I'm kinda good at that one myself," Bullock said.

In the morning, Tillman and Bullock rode west along the Little Missouri River for about ten miles, when Tillman held up his right hand and they stopped.

"What is it, Sam?" Bullock said softly.

"Listen," Tillman whispered. "From that thicket of trees to the left."

They dismounted, grabbed their Winchesters, and walked toward the thicket of trees.

"It's my own fault," a man's voice said. "My own damn fault."

Tillman and Bullock walked closer and came up behind the man. His back was to them as he sat in front of a small campfire. He was dressed in tan buckskin, including buckskin hat and gloves.

"What is your own damn fault?" Tillman said.

Startled, the man turned around. He wore rimless spectacles that nearly fell off his nose from the sudden movement.

"Who are you?" the man said as he adjusted his spectacles.

"Marshal Sam Tillman. This is Deputy Marshal Seth Bullock," Tillman said.

"I'm Theodore Roosevelt, Deputy Sheriff of Medora," Roosevelt said.

"Stand up there, Deputy," Tillman said.

Roosevelt stood.

"What's that around your waist?" Tillman said.

"A Smith and Wesson .38," Roosevelt said.

"I have two questions," Tillman said. "The first is, what in the hell are you dressed up for?"

Bullock started to laugh.

"These are my frontiersmen's clothing," Roosevelt said.

Bullock laughed so hard, he nearly slipped and fell.

"Seth, please," Tillman said. "Now Deputy Roosevelt, where did you get the idea for that getup, from some dime novel?"

"From a store in New York City that sells clothing for adventure," Roosevelt said.

"Adventure," Bullock said and collapsed to the ground in a fit of laughter.

"I don't see what is so funny about my

—" Roosevelt said.

"My second question is what the hell are you doing out here alone?" Tillman said.

"I am in pursuit of nine scoundrels who absconded with my riverboat off the Little Missouri River," Roosevelt said.

Still on the ground, Bullock looked at Tillman. "What did he say?"

"They stole his boat," Tillman said. "Deputy Roosevelt, let's put on a pot of coffee and have us a talk."

Tillman sipped coffee and looked across the campfire at Roosevelt.

"What kind of boat is this they stole from you?" Tillman said.

"A riverboat," Roosevelt said. "I use it for transporting pelts and goods."

"What you said earlier about it being your fault, what were you talking about?" Tillman said.

"I left my boat unguarded and unsecured overnight," Roosevelt said. "I figured to secure it in the morning. It was my fault for being lazy."

"Lesson taught," Bullock said. "Lesson learned."

"Those nine men are dangerous outlaws, Deputy," Tillman said. "What were you planning to do if you caught up with them, one man against nine?"

"I guess I didn't quite think this through all the way," Roosevelt said.

"No offense, Deputy, but one look at your getup, and they'd likely laugh themselves to death," Bullock said.

"Mind me asking where you're from, Deputy?" Tillman said.

"New York City."

Tillman and Bullock grinned at each other.

"I know what you fellows are thinking, but I've traveled a great deal and even abroad. I felt it was time to see the west, so here I came," Roosevelt said.

"I've seen you before," Tillman said. "In the newspapers. I read the speech you made at a Chicago convention in the newspapers. A fine speech."

"I read that myself," Bullock said. "That was a fine speech."

"Right now I have more pressing matters. I have to retrieve my boat," Roosevelt said.

"This river is six hundred miles long, and we ain't going to catch them tonight. It will be dark soon. Let's make camp," Bullock said.

Around the campfire, Tillman, Bullock, and Roosevelt ate a supper of beef stew with beans and thick, crusty bread.

"You fellows brought much better food than I did," Roosevelt said. "And the tent looks rather comfortable."

"We've been doing this kind of work longer than you, I think," Bullock said.

"How long do you suppose before we catch up to those men?" Roosevelt said.

"A few days. Maybe tomorrow," Bullock said.

"It's a river, Mr. Roosevelt, so eventually they will run out of water," Tillman said.

Bullock grinned while Roosevelt appeared befuddled.

"Why, yes, that's true. Eventually they will run out of water," Roosevelt said.

Tillman and Bullock started to laugh. After a few seconds, Roosevelt joined in.

"God help us," Tillman said.

Two days later, riding north along the Little Missouri River, Tillman said, "Hold up," and dismounted.

Tillman inspected the many sets of tracks in the soft earth and mud.

"They came ashore here," Tillman said. "Probably to hunt game."

"How long ago?" Roosevelt said.

"Yesterday," Tillman said.

Tillman mounted his horse. "We should

catch them sometime tomorrow," he said.

Tillman cooked supper while Bullock and Roosevelt assembled the tent and saw to the horses and mule.

As they ate, Roosevelt said, "I guess I was foolish going after them alone, nine to one, but it occurred to me that three to one isn't much better odds."

"Deputy Roosevelt, never underestimate the power of the element of surprise," Tillman said. "Think of us as lions stalking prey."

"I will remember that for future use," Roosevelt said.

"The election in eighty-four, you took the loss hard," Tillman said. "Is that why you came west? To get away from all that?"

"More or less. Politics is a dirty business," Roosevelt said. "And besides, I really do love the west and the outdoors."

"Maybe so, Deputy Roosevelt, but for God's sake, buy yourself some decent clothes," Tillman said.

The following afternoon, riding single file with Tillman in the lead, Tillman suddenly held up his hand and then dismounted.

Bullock and Roosevelt dismounted and joined Tillman.

"What?" Bullock said.

"Look at the river," Tillman said.

Large chunks of ice had drifted west on the water and had caused an ice jam.

Tillman removed his Winchester from the saddle.

"I'll be back in a few minutes," he said.

Tillman walked off along the river.

"Should we go with him?" Roosevelt said to Bullock.

"That's one man you don't need to worry about, Deputy," Bullock said.

Tillman walked about two hundred feet into the thicket of trees along the river. There he saw a large riverboat stuck in chunks of ice that blocked it from traveling any further.

Nine men were on deck, talking and drinking.

Tillman returned to Bullock and Roosevelt.

"The boat is, as we figured, stuck in ice," Tillman said. "I didn't see their horses. Is there room below the deck for the horses?"

"For at least a dozen or more, if the men stay on top," Roosevelt said.

"All right, let's walk the horses and tie them out of sight," Tillman said.

They brought the horses to safety, grabbed their Winchesters, and took a position a hundred feet from the riverboat.

"I count the nine we came for," Bullock said.

"To our three," Roosevelt said.

"It will be dark in two hours. We can't wait. We'll have to take them now," Tillman said.

"Take them . . . how?" Roosevelt said.

"Spread out about thirty feet. I'll take center. Get good cover," Tillman said. "They'll likely shoot first and talk later."

Bullock and Roosevelt spread out about thirty feet and took cover behind trees.

"You on the boat! You are surrounded by a posse of marshals. Surrender your weapons and come out, and nobody has to get shot," Tillman shouted.

There was a long moment of silence before a man responded from the boat.

"We don't believe you got no posse of marshals," the man shouted. "And even if you do, we don't care."

"I won't say it again. Surrender your weapons and come out peacefully. What is your answer?" Tillman shouted.

"This," the man shouted.

The nine outlaws opened fire. Tillman, Bullock, and Roosevelt hugged the ground behind the trees.

"What do you think of our answer, Marshal?" an outlaw shouted.

"You've run aground. You're trapped in the ice. You got nowhere to go. You can't escape," Tillman shouted.

"Maybe not, but we sure as hell can kill you," an outlaw shouted.

The nine outlaws opened fire again, and a barrage of bullets struck the trees and dirt as Tillman, Bullock, and Roosevelt hugged the ground again.

"Are you still alive, Marshal?" a man shouted. "You want some more?"

"By God, I've had enough of these assholes," Tillman said.

Tillman stood, turned, and walked toward his horse.

"Marshal Tillman, what are you doing?" Roosevelt said. "Marshal Bullock, what is he doing?"

"I don't know. Give him some cover though," Bullock said.

Bullock and Roosevelt fired their Winchesters at the boat. They stopped firing when Tillman appeared atop his horse with his Colt revolver in his right hand and a spare Colt in his waistband.

"Sam?" Bullock said.

Tillman cracked the reins and raced his horse directly to the embankment and to the shock of the outlaws on board the boat.

Then Tillman jumped the railing and landed on the deck.

The outlaws in the boat were astonished by what they'd just witnessed. Before they could react, Tillman opened fire. In a matter of seconds, Tillman shot six men dead, then dropped the Colt and grabbed the spare from his waistband.

The remaining three outlaws stared in shock at Tillman as he cocked the Colt and took aim at them.

"What's it going to be?" Tillman said. "Six dead or nine?"

The three men dropped their rifles.

"By God, six dead men, and for what? So you can rustle cows and steal a man's boat? Put your bellies on the deck, hands on your head," Tillman said.

The three outlaws got on their bellies.

Tillman dismounted as Bullock and Roosevelt boarded the riverboat.

"Holy shit, Sam," Bullock said.

Roosevelt looked at the six dead outlaws. "Good God," he said.

"Element of surprise, Deputy Roosevelt," Tillman said. He looked at the three outlaws. "Grab your shovels. You got some digging to do."

A week later, after the ice melted and freed

up the river, Roosevelt piloted his riverboat east along the Little Missouri River to Medora.

The citizens of Medora were shocked at the sight of Roosevelt docking the riverboat at the landing.

"Deputy Roosevelt, have you a jail where we can lock these three up and a place where Seth and I can stay the night?" Tillman said. "And maybe a warm saloon where we can have us a well-earned drink?"

The incident became the talk of the town and would later be written up in a dime novel as *Roosevelt and the River Boat Thieves.*

Tillman and Bullock stayed the night at Roosevelt's cabin. In the morning, Bullock returned to Deadwood, while Tillman took the three living outlaws to Montana for trial.

1901

Tillman closed the book after reading the final chapter and removed his reading glasses. He was about to wave to the waiter when Brass showed up at the table with two fresh cups of coffee.

"May I sit?" Brass said.

"Help yourself."

Brass took a chair. "Thanks."

"I'm going to follow you to the end of the

line, wherever that is," Brass said. "I witnessed you with some very famous and remarkable people, Marshal, and yet you prefer to stay in the background."

"That's because I prefer the background," Tillman said. "Is there something wrong with that?"

"No," Brass said and looked at the dime novel on the table. "But if there is more to a public story than the public is aware of, it's my job to make them aware."

"Even if it's nobody's damned business," Tillman said.

"The public has a right to know the full story, especially if the story glorifies someone," Brass said. "The public has the right to know if the person being glorified is worthy of adulation."

"At the expense of people who just want to mind their own business?" Tillman said. "The First Amendment is not the only one, you know."

"You make a compelling argument," Brass said.

"But, you're going to follow me around anyway?" Tillman said.

"It's my job," Brass said.

"Do me a favor and don't get in my way," Tillman said. "You might find yourself with lead in more places than that pencil in your shirt pocket there."

CHAPTER TWENTY-EIGHT

1901

Tillman read a newspaper beside a window in a riding car. He quietly smoked his pipe as he read a sports story written by Bat Masterson.

Seated across the aisle, Brass made notes in his book and then made another sketch.

Both men looked up when a conductor passed through.

"What time do we reach Laramie?" Tillman said.

"About an hour," the conductor said.

"Obliged," Tillman said.

Brass looked at Tillman as Tillman returned to reading his newspaper.

1898

In late April, the headline in every newspaper in the country was the Spanish attack on the American armored cruiser the USS Maine in Havana Harbor.

Of the 355 souls on board, only 94 survived the surprise attack.

Like most Americans, Tillman was concerned about what might happen next.

In early May, while having dinner with Alice at home, a telegram was delivered to Tillman by special courier.

"What does it say?" Alice said.

"I'm to travel to Washington to discuss private details concerning the attack on the Maine," Tillman said.

"Whatever for?" Alice said.

"I guess I'll find out," Tillman said.

"When are you going to retire, Sam?" Alice said. "You're too damned old for this kind of work now."

"And sit in a rocking chair on the porch while my sons do all the work?" Tillman said. "Not yet, baby sister. I'll let you know when."

Alice sighed. "I best go pack your gear."

When Tillman arrived in Washington, he expected a meeting with Post and the director of the Marshals Service. He was surprised to find Ted Roosevelt in the office.

At the time, Roosevelt was serving as Assistant Secretary of the Navy.

"Ted, why am I not surprised to see you here?" Tillman said.

"Sam, I need you," Roosevelt said. "I've resigned my position with the navy. I aim to head up a volunteer division of a thousand troops and will lead them into battle in Cuba."

"You're crazy," Tillman said.

"That's what McKinley said, but Roosevelt got him to change his mind," Post said with a grin.

"One thousand volunteers, Sam, and they all need training," Roosevelt said. "I need you to help me, Sam. I can't train these men alone. I need your experience and your knowledge. I've asked Seth, too. He's agreed to help, but he's a lawman and not a soldier."

Tillman looked at Post.

"It's up to you, Sam, but I've already told Ted you can't go to Cuba," Post said.

"Three weeks to a month is what I ask, Sam," Roosevelt said. "In San Antoine, Texas."

"Can I go home and get my horse first?" Tillman said.

Of the one thousand volunteers, only a handful had actual military service and none of it combat-related. Most were cowboys, sheriffs, athletes, hunters, coal miners, and businessmen.

Some were decent shots. None were ready for war.

For weeks, Tillman and Bullock instructed the volunteers on marksmanship with long guns and revolvers.

The men drilled and practiced military maneuvers from sunup to sundown until they actually resembled a fighting force.

Tillman, Roosevelt, and Bullock shared a room in the barracks.

Bullock opened a bottle of bourbon and poured three drinks. "The men are coming along, Ted. A few more weeks and they'll be ready," he said.

"A few more weeks and we'll be in Cuba," Roosevelt said.

"They're good men," Tillman said. "They'll do their duty."

"I know," Roosevelt said. "Sam, I need a favor."

"Being here wet-nursing these amateurs isn't enough of a favor?" Bullock said.

"I'm serious," Roosevelt said.

"If I can," Tillman said.

"The men will all be on foot," Roosevelt said. "I want to lead the charge on horseback."

"You'd be the first one shot," Bullock said.

"Not if Sam teaches me how not to be," Roosevelt said.

"Ted, I don't think this is wise idea," Tillman said.

"I'm going to do it anyway, Sam," Roosevelt said. "You might as well show me how and give me a fighting chance at coming home alive."

Tillman nodded and then tossed back his drink.

"We'll work on it," Tillman said.

Sitting atop Blue, Tillman had a firm grip on the reins with his left hand.

"Your horse needs to know that you're in charge," Tillman said. "If your horse senses panic in you, your horse will panic. So at all cost, remain calm and in control. Your horse will respond in kind."

Tillman tugged the reins to the right, and Blue responded.

"Your horse will go where you direct it," Tillman said. "The trick is to get your horse to ignore the bullets, bombs, and noise and stay focused."

"How do I do that?" Roosevelt said.

"By doing the exact same thing," Tillman said. "Mount up, Colonel Roosevelt."

Roosevelt mounted the saddle.

"Those six targets represent six of the enemy," Tillman said.

Six bottles rested on six, six-foot-high

posts set in a zigzag pattern twenty feet apart.

"Your horse and you are one and the same," Tillman said. "He's an extension of you, and you're an extension of him. You both work together, like a couple dancing a waltz."

Tillman drew his Colt, cocked it, then yanked the reins and Blue took off running.

Tillman shot the first bottle and then yanked Blue to the left, shot another bottle, turned Blue to the right, and shot another bottle. Then he shot the remaining three bottles, all the while zigzagging Blue through the posts.

On the sidelines, Bullock said, "Remind you of anything, Ted?"

"I'm never going to live that damned riverboat incident down, am I?" Roosevelt said.

"Seth, set up another six bottles so Ted can have a go," Tillman said.

After a week of practice, Roosevelt was able to maneuver the posts, fire six shots, and actually hit two of the bottles.

A week later, Roosevelt managed to hit three of the bottles while zigzagging through the course.

"I'm afraid I'll never be as good as you,

Sam," Roosevelt said.

"Don't worry about that," Tillman said. "Your men will be looking to you for leadership. Give it to them. Carry a second revolver, and when the first is empty, grab the second. When that's empty, draw your sword and keep charging forward. Keep your horse moving right and left, but always forward. And show no fear. Your men will sense it if you show fear and respond to your fear. Then you'll lose the battle, and they will lose their lives."

Roosevelt nodded.

"Let's practice charging," Tillman said.

"Charging what?" Roosevelt said.

Bullock rolled his eyes. "Hold on. I'll get a red cape and wave it at you, Ted," he said.

"Well, Sam, tomorrow we ship out for Cuba," Roosevelt said. "I wish I had the hard bark on me that you have on you."

"Lead your men, Ted," Tillman said. "Remember this one thing. On the battlefield, your men need leadership. Do whatever it takes to lead them into battle. Don't waver, don't show fear in the face of the enemy, and always show them you're in charge."

Roosevelt nodded.

"Let's have a drink," Bullock said.

Bullock filled three small glasses with whiskey and gave one each to Roosevelt and Tillman.

"To Cuba," Bullock said.

"To Teddy Roosevelt," Tillman said. "To victory in Cuba."

1901

Walking through the car, the conductor shouted, "Laramie. The stop is Laramie."

Tillman stood and left the newspaper on the seat. He looked at Brass.

"Are you coming, Mr. Brass?" Tillman said.

Brass stood and followed Tillman to the door where they waited for the train to stop at the station.

CHAPTER TWENTY-NINE

Laramie, Wyoming, 1901
Tillman led Blue by the reins along the platform. Brass walked beside him.

At the edge of the platform, Tillman paused to read a plaque mounted to the wall of the depot.

Tillman read the plaque aloud.

"The first passengers of the Union Pacific left Laramie on May fourth, 1868," Tillman said. "Someday they'll have to correct that."

"Correct what?" Brass said.

"It's May tenth," Tillman said. "Not May fourth."

"How do you know?" Brass said.

"Because I was here," Tillman said. "And helped build this town."

Brass took out his notebook to scribble a note. When he looked up, Tillman and Blue were in the street, walking away. Brass had to scurry to catch up to them.

"Look around you, son. What do you see?

Stores and shops, fine brick buildings and women in the latest dresses from Chicago. It wasn't so long ago a man could get shot for spitting the wrong way in Laramie," Tillman said.

Tillman led Blue and Brass to the end of a block and paused.

"That tall red brick building there in the distance, that's a college, of all things," Tillman said.

Brass looked at the college and then around him at the sidewalks.

"People are watching us," Brass said.

"Two things folks in Laramie aren't used to seeing these days. As you can tell by all the damned buggies, people don't see many men on horseback anymore," Tillman said.

Brass looked at several buggies in the street.

"And the other thing they don't see much of anymore is a man carrying a gun in plain sight," Tillman said.

"Is that why people are clearing the sidewalks?" Brass said.

"I expect so. Come on, Mr. Brass," Tillman said and started walking again.

Tillman led Blue and Brass to the center of town, where Tillman paused to watch a Laramie deputy enter a saloon.

They walked to the saloon, and Tillman

looked at the etched glass window. The words *Bucket of Blood Saloon* were carved into the glass.

"This saloon has been here since 1868. I know, because I was here the day it opened," Tillman said.

Tillman tethered Blue to the hitching post and then looked at Brass.

"Now stay the hell out of the way, and you just might not get shot," Tillman said.

Tillman entered the crowded saloon, walked to the bar, and stood directly behind the deputy.

The saloon immediately went silent.

"Don't move, son. I'm United States Marshal Sam Tillman, and I'm here to relieve Town Marshal John Sale of his duties. Answer me a question, son. Do you wish to live or die?" Tillman said.

"I don't want to die, Marshal," the deputy said.

"Put your Smith and Wesson on the bar, son," Tillman said.

The deputy slowly withdrew the heavy revolver from its holster and placed it on the bar.

Tillman waved the bartender over.

"Barkeep, empty the deputy's weapon and place it under the bar," Tillman said.

"Marshal, I don't want to get involved,"

the bartender said.

"Did that sound like a question to   b
Tillman said. "Do it."

The bartender picked up the de
revolver, removed the six shells, and p   a
revolver under the bar.   t

"Now turn around, Deputy," Tillma

Slowly, the deputy turned aroun   l
faced Tillman.   c

"How old are you, son?" Tillman sa

"Twenty-three," the deputy said.

"Ever kill a man?" Tillman said.

"No, sir."

"Ever use that piece of yours for any
besides target practice?" Tillman said.

"No, sir."

"Where is Marshal Sale right now?"
man said.

"At the office," the deputy said.

"How many with him?" Tillman said.

"Four other deputies," the deputy sai

"How do you know that?" Tillman sa

"We always have a meeting at five o'cl
It's five o'clock. I was about to join t
when you showed up. We always take o
pot of coffee from the saloon," the dep
said. "That's what I was waiting on."

"How long have you been a deputy, so
Tillman said.

"Three months."

"Three whole months, huh? Bartender, bring me some rope and a bar towel," Tillman said.

The bartender reached under the bar for a towel. "I have to go to the back room for the rope," he said.

Tillman took the towel. "Stay right there, barkeep. Where I can see you until I figure out who is on whose side."

"Nobody in the room has any love for Marshal Sale," the bartender said. "Least of all me."

"All right, get me some rope," Tillman said. He looked at the deputy. "You, have a seat over there."

The deputy pulled out an empty chair at a table and sat.

The bartender returned with a long piece of rope and handed it to Tillman.

"A couple of you men tie his hands and legs to the chair and stuff this towel in his mouth," Tillman said.

"What are you going to do, Marshal?" the deputy said.

"What I said I was going to do," Tillman said.

"Sale is awful mean and very fast with his gun, Marshal," the deputy said.

"That's my concern now, son," Tillman said.

While two men tied the deputy's hands and legs to the chair, Tillman turned to the bartender.

"Barkeep, let me have a shot of your best bourbon whiskey. While I drink it, you can tell me what's been going on around here," Tillman said.

The bartender filled a shot glass with whiskey and set it before Tillman.

"You can start any time," Tillman said as he took a sip of whiskey.

The bartender filled a shot glass, picked it up, and gulped it down. "Sale is plumb crazy, Marshal. He's taken over the whole damn town. The saloons can't open until four, and gambling isn't allowed until eight. Everybody must attend church on Sunday, even if they don't want to. Shopkeepers and saloons have to pay him for protection or risk having a fire during the night. The sheriff tried to stop him, and that started a war in the streets. Sale killed the sheriff and ran the deputies out of town. He . . ."

"That's enough," Tillman said.

Tillman tossed down his drink, turned around, and looked at the fifty or so men in the saloon. Brass was against the wall, making notes in his notepad.

"Nobody is to move from this room," Tillman said.

"What are you going to do, Marshal?" the bartender said.

"I'm going to have another drink. While I'm doing that you are going to mosey on across the street and deliver a message to Marshal Sale," Tillman said.

"What do you want me to tell him?" the bartender said as he filled Tillman's shot glass.

"Tell him this. Tell him Marshal Sam Tillman will be outside in five minutes to remove him from office," Tillman said.

"Alone?" the bartender said.

"Unless you want to strap on a gun and accompany me," Tillman said.

"No, sir, I don't think so," the bartender said.

"Best do it right now," Tillman said.

The bartender came out from behind the bar and slowly walked to the swinging doors. He paused at the doors, then opened them and stepped outside.

Tillman quietly sipped his drink and looked at the patrons. Most gazed at their tables and the floor. Not one of them made eye contact with him.

Except for Brass, who stared at Tillman.

Tillman lifted the shot glass to Brass, downed the bourbon, and then gently set the glass down on the bar.

"Some of you men carry the deputy here to a back room and make sure the door is locked," Tillman said.

Several men carried the deputy to the back room and locked the door.

"Well, best get to it," Tillman said.

Tillman placed two dollars on the bar and turned around. He walked to the swinging doors and exited the saloon.

Against the wall, Brass turned to look out the window. Every person in the saloon ran to the windows and looked out.

On the wood sidewalk, Tillman stepped down and stood beside Blue. He rubbed Blue's neck for a moment, then removed his spare Colt revolver from a saddlebag and stuck it in his belt.

He looked at the town marshal's office across the street.

Finally, the bartender emerged from the town marshal's office and ran back to the saloon, passed Tillman, and entered it.

Tillman took Blue by the reins, mounted the saddle, and rubbed Blue's neck.

"Easy, boy. You know what to do. We've done it many times before," Tillman said.

With the afternoon sun at his back, Tillman rode Blue to the center of the street.

The door to the town marshal's office opened. Four deputies filed out and stood on the sidewalk. Each deputy carried a Winchester rifle besides a sidearm.

The deputies stood there watching Tillman until John Sale slowly emerged. Sale also carried a Winchester rifle and had a Smith and Wesson .44 holstered on his right hip.

Sale was a tall, hard-looking man with a dark mustache.

Atop Blue, Tillman removed the lash from his Colt.

Sale looked directly at Tillman. A twisted little smile crossed his lips.

"Son of a bitch if it ain't really you, Sam Tillman," Sale said.

"It's me," Tillman said.

"What's all this crap the barkeep said about you relieving me of my badge?" Sale said.

"I gave it to you, son. I can take it away," Tillman said.

"You can't do that, Sam. Not to me," Sale said.

"At the request of the United States government I can and I will," Tillman said.

"I can't allow that, Sam," Sale said.

"I'm afraid you have no say in the matter anymore, John. The decision has already been made," Tillman said.

Sale grinned. "Look around you, Sam. I

have made this the safest town in the state. No killings, no crime, no guns, and it's because of me. People go to church here, Sam. All of them. Because of me," he said.

"Out of fear, John. You swore an oath to uphold the federal law inside the limits of Laramie, not to make your own laws. I am deeply troubled that you fail to understand the difference," Tillman said.

Sale chuckled. "It seems to me you're all alone, Sam. Why don't you just ride out before you get killed?" he said.

"I'll have your badge, John," Tillman said.

"You're an old man now, Sam. And I'm not, and you taught me well," Sale said.

"I taught you to shoot, that is true. But I failed to teach you when to shoot. Worse, I failed to teach you how to be a man," Tillman said.

"I guess that's it then, Sam, because I'm not giving you my badge," Sale said.

Tillman looked at the four deputies.

"You deputies, if you don't want to get killed, drop the rifles and surrender your sidearms. I promise no man will be harmed if he surrenders peacefully," Tillman said.

Sale snickered.

Tillman sighed heavily.

There was a quiet moment when Tillman and Sale made eye contact.

"Last chance to surrender your badge, John," Tillman said.

"You go to hell, Sam Tillman," Sale said.

Tillman stared at Sale.

"Fan out, men. He's just one old man on a tuckered-out old horse," Sale said.

The moment the first deputy moved, Tillman raced Blue diagonally across the street, pulled his Colt, and shot the deputy dead with a bullet to the heart.

Sale and the remaining three deputies didn't even have time to move before Tillman raced Blue back across the street and shot another deputy dead.

Sale and his remaining two deputies cocked their Winchesters and attempted to take aim at Tillman.

In the two seconds it took them to cock the levers and aim the rifles, Tillman was in motion again, racing Blue directly at Sale and the deputies.

They fired and missed Tillman by ten feet.

Tillman fired his Colt without aiming, knowing the bullet would go where he pointed it, and shot another deputy dead at Sale's feet.

The remaining deputy looked at Tillman atop the tall horse, dropped his Winchester to the street, turned, and ran away.

Sale turned and shot the deputy in the back.

"You damn coward," Sale shouted.

When Sale turned back around, Tillman had dismounted and was facing him from a distance of twenty feet. Tillman's Colt was holstered.

"I'll have that badge now, John," Tillman said.

Sale grinned at Tillman.

"I don't want to kill you, son. But I will have that badge before I leave this town," Tillman said.

"Come and take it then, Sam," Sale said. "If you're able."

Sale tossed his rifle to the street. A second of quiet ensued, and time seemed to freeze for several moments.

Then Sale reached for his large Smith and Wesson. Before he cleared the holster, Tillman was aiming his Colt directly at Sale's heart.

"Holster it and give me that badge, John," Tillman said.

Sale stared at Tillman. Slowly, a thin smile crossed Sale's lips.

"You go straight to hell, Sam Tillman," Sale said.

"Don't do it, son. You don't have to do this," Tillman said.

"I have to, Sam. It's gone too far, and the whole town is watching. I have no choice," Sale said.

"I know," Tillman said.

"Goodbye, Sam," Sale said.

"Goodbye, John," Tillman said.

Sale cleared his holster and Tillman shot him in the chest, dead center.

The Smith and Wesson dropped from Sale's hand as he fell to his knees and then slumped to the street.

Tillman sighed openly as he holstered his Colt and then walked to Sale.

Sale was still alive and Tillman knelt down beside him and cradled his head.

"Oh, Sam, I don't want to die," Sale said.

Tillman looked at Sale with great sadness in his eyes.

"I know, son. I know," Tillman said.

A moment later, Sale's eyes closed and he drew his final breath.

Tillman stood, retrieved Blue, and walked him back to the saloon. There he tethered Blue to the hitching post.

Every patron, including the bartender and Brass, were at the windows.

No one said a word as Tillman entered the saloon, walked to the bar, and poured himself a drink. He turned and faced the crowd.

"I will stay until the team of marshals arrive with the new sheriff, about three days from now. Do you have an undertaker?" Tillman said.

"Yes," the bartender said.

"Get him," Tillman said.

The bartender nodded and rushed out of the saloon.

Tillman took his drink to a table, sat, and took out his pipe. He stuffed it with tobacco from his pouch and lit it with a wood match.

Brass cautiously approached Tillman and sat opposite him at the table.

"You . . . you killed them all," Brass said.

Tillman took a small sip of his drink and looked at Brass.

"And you think I'm proud of that?" Tillman said.

Brass stood and walked to the bar and poured himself a drink. His hands shook a bit as he lifted the glass to sip.

The bartender returned with a man who was wearing a dark suit. The man paused and looked at the fifty or so people standing along the walls. The bartender returned to the bar, poured a drink, and gulped it down.

Tillman looked at the man. "Are you the undertaker?" he said.

"I am. Name is Johnson."

"Have you a paper and pencil, Mr. Johnson?" Tillman said.

Johnson nodded.

"Please have a seat and take pencil to paper," Tillman said.

Johnson sat opposite Tillman and took out a pencil and a small pad.

"I want the body of John Sale properly seen to and placed into the best coffin you have. You are to ship the coffin to his mother, my sister, Alice Sale-Tillman at the Tillman Ranch in Montana. You got that?" Tillman said.

Johnson stared at Tillman.

"Mr. Johnson, do you got that?" Tillman said.

"I . . . yeah. Yes I got it, Marshal," Johnson said.

"Good," Tillman said. "I'll make payment in cash before I leave town."

Tillman stood up from the table and slowly walked out of the saloon.

No one moved. Not a sound was made until Tillman reached the street. Then everyone rushed to the windows.

Everyone except Brass.

At the bar, Brass took out his notebook and stared at it. Then he tore out pages, ripped them to shreds, and left them on the bar.

Chapter Thirty

Montana, 1901

"Well, boys, it's going to take me a day and a half to reach Miles City," Post said. "I'd best be on my way."

Post, Alice, Glen, and Jake were on the porch after breakfast.

"We'll ride along with you a ways," Glen said.

"All right," Post said. He turned to Alice. "I hope I didn't put you out too much, Alice."

"Nonsense," Alice said. "I enjoyed your company."

Alice gave Post a warm hug, and then Post walked down the steps and got into his buggy.

"We'll be back," Glen said to Alice.

Tillman rode Blue at a leisurely pace along the road leading to his ranch.

The spring sun was warm on his back,

and Blue moved along with a youthful gate in his step.

Tillman slowed Blue to a stop when he noticed something far in the distance. He dug out the binoculars from a saddlebag, focused them, and said aloud, "Well, look at this, boy. We got us a welcoming committee."

Tillman replaced the binoculars and tugged on the reins.

"Let's go say hello," Tillman said.

ABOUT THE AUTHOR

Ethan J. Wolfe is the author of a dozen historical western novels, including the popular series, The Regulator.